COMICS

Presents

Volume 1

Collecting
Brute #0 - #3

T. Preston Squire • Owen Keenan

Cover Art: Loc Nguyen
Variant Cover Art (page 33): Dixie Alvarez
Variant Cover Art (page 116): Rob Thibodeau
Interior Design: Davor Dramikanin

Brute The toughest 'Teddy Bear'
in the Galaxy #0-#3

Writer/Creator: T. Preston Squire

Line Art: Owen Keenan

Color Art: Brooke Newhart

Lettering: Owen Keenan

KAW!
GRAWK!
THWIP!
THWIP!

Lom the Last

Artist / Dialogue / Creator: Owen Keenan

Captions: T. Preston Squire

STAY UP TO DATE WITH WHAT'S HAPPENING WITH
BRUTE AND THE CREATIVE TEAM
EXCLUSIVE SNEAK-PEAKS, ART AND INSIGHTS
ENROLL AT
BRUTECOMIC.COM/OFFER
STAY IN TOUCH!
OR I'LL COME LOOKING FOR YA.
See you there!

What if... the toughest guy in the galaxy just happened to look like... a teddy bear?

Brute, of course, is the answer. When I'm at comic cons, the number one question I'm asked is when did I start working on Brute. The answer to that question is twofold. Part one: When did Brute the character come into being, and part two: when did Brute the comic begin?

To answer the first question, we have to time travel all the way back to 1988 (ish) when I was a 'Dungeon Master' (DM) for a weekly role-playing group made up of an ever-rotating group of friends and my brothers. Despite being a 'DM,' we didn't play D&D – we usually played a Marvel Superheroes RPG using characters of our own creations in a universe of my own creation (the genesis of the 'Bruteverse').

In one long epic campaign, the 'heroes,' in this case intergalactic bounty hunters and mercenaries who were working together to kill an unkillable target, needed some competition. Enter another group of alien bounty hunters who were

gunning for the same target. Not outright enemies, but certainly not above screwing them over if it meant they'd be closer to bagging the bounty.

This crew consisted of some of the characters you're about to meet, like the porcupinian Captain Vanguard, and the giant plantis Rintax, as well as the dastardly human Great Grey, a shapeshifting doppleganger, and of course, Brute. But why Brute? Why a teddy bear? Well, he's not literally a teddy bear; he just happens to resemble one, and it's because of the intense gravity on his cold home world.

I always like to usurp expectations, and because every group always has their super-strong character (Superman in the Justice League, Thor in Avengers, Colossus in X-Men, Sasquatch in Alpha Flight, etc.) and Rintax, a towering plant-person seems like that obvious threat they'd attack first, I thought let's flip this script. So I made Rintax a pacifist and created a completely harmless-looking 'joke' character, sure to be overlooked, who'd then completely blindside them as they were dealing with the others.

It worked brilliantly, of course, and everyone loved this tough guy teddy bear who just beat the snot out of them. He was such a fun character; I knew I had to do a book about him. However, that book proved elusive. I tried many times, in comic form, and in novel form, to craft a compelling story, but it just didn't have the same appeal somehow.

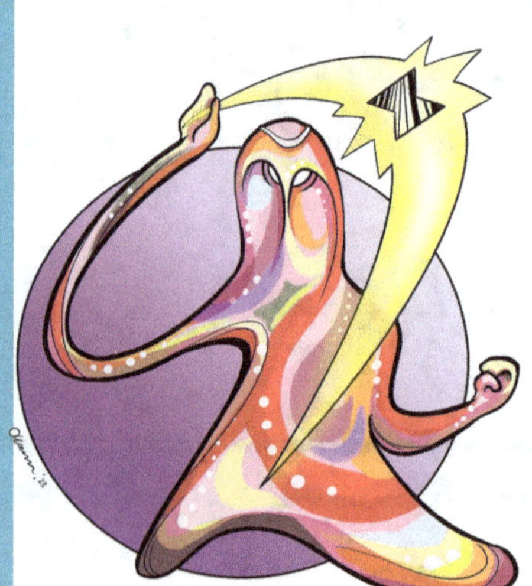

Over these years, I added Rose, a human character I'd made back in the '70s, and the glob 'Stretch' to the team (dropping Great Gray and the doppleganger) and much later, the oviraptor-like Drifter (a merging of another story idea of an evolved dinosaur world). And while an entertaining cast of misfits, something still wasn't right. Brute, as cool and lovable as he is, just wasn't all that likable as the protagonist. In short, early Brute – is a jerk.

Around 2018, I obtained new writing software, and just for fun, to try it out, I decided to take another stab at Brute. But this time, instead of telling Brute's origin, I told Rose's. It was like that moment in the Sixth Sense (spoiler alert) when you realize that Bruce Willis' character is a ghost, and suddenly every little 'off' thing in the movie slips into making complete sense. Suddenly, it worked. Everything worked! Rose, the only human in a completely alien galaxy, became the reader's way of discovering this weird and wonderful world. And Rose, with her mix of insecurities, heart, and never-give-up attitude, was immensely likable. Like a joyful three-legged dog, you can't help but want to see her succeed.

Over the next two years, I scripted the first seven issues of a Brute series, without any real plan as to what to do with them. Then out-of-the-blue, a childhood friend looked me up to ask me if I'd help him create a comic idea he now suddenly had time to work on. 'Sure,' I said, 'but here's what I'm working on...' and dropped the scripts on him. Owen LOVED them. And soon, we'd create a trial comic for an anthology comic called 'Yeet!' (Issue #36 for you collectors of rare oddities).

Reception was good, so we continued to do two more. Further encouraged that Brute had a future, we began work on our comic series, and Brute – Toughest Guy in the Galaxy was born.

You'll find those original short stories collected into Brute #0, which despite coming first sequentially, would actually happen around the Brute #13 mark – so it's a sneak peek of what's to come in a way (although, aside from Brute & Rose ending up with Brute's old buddy Vanguard somehow, there's no 'spoilers' here).

Over the next three years, we'd release Brute #1, #2, and #3 and sell hundreds of copies at conventions all over our native Ontario, Canada. While successful, the reach was just too small, so we decided to compile all four issues, plus some added exclusive content and Chapter 1 of a new eSq character, 'Lom the Last' and release them all between the covers of this book you're holding.

It's our hope that this compilation and format will be able to reach a much wider audience who can discover Brute, Rose, and company for the first time, but certainly not the last time. We've many more stories to come!

By the Essence,

T. Preston Squire

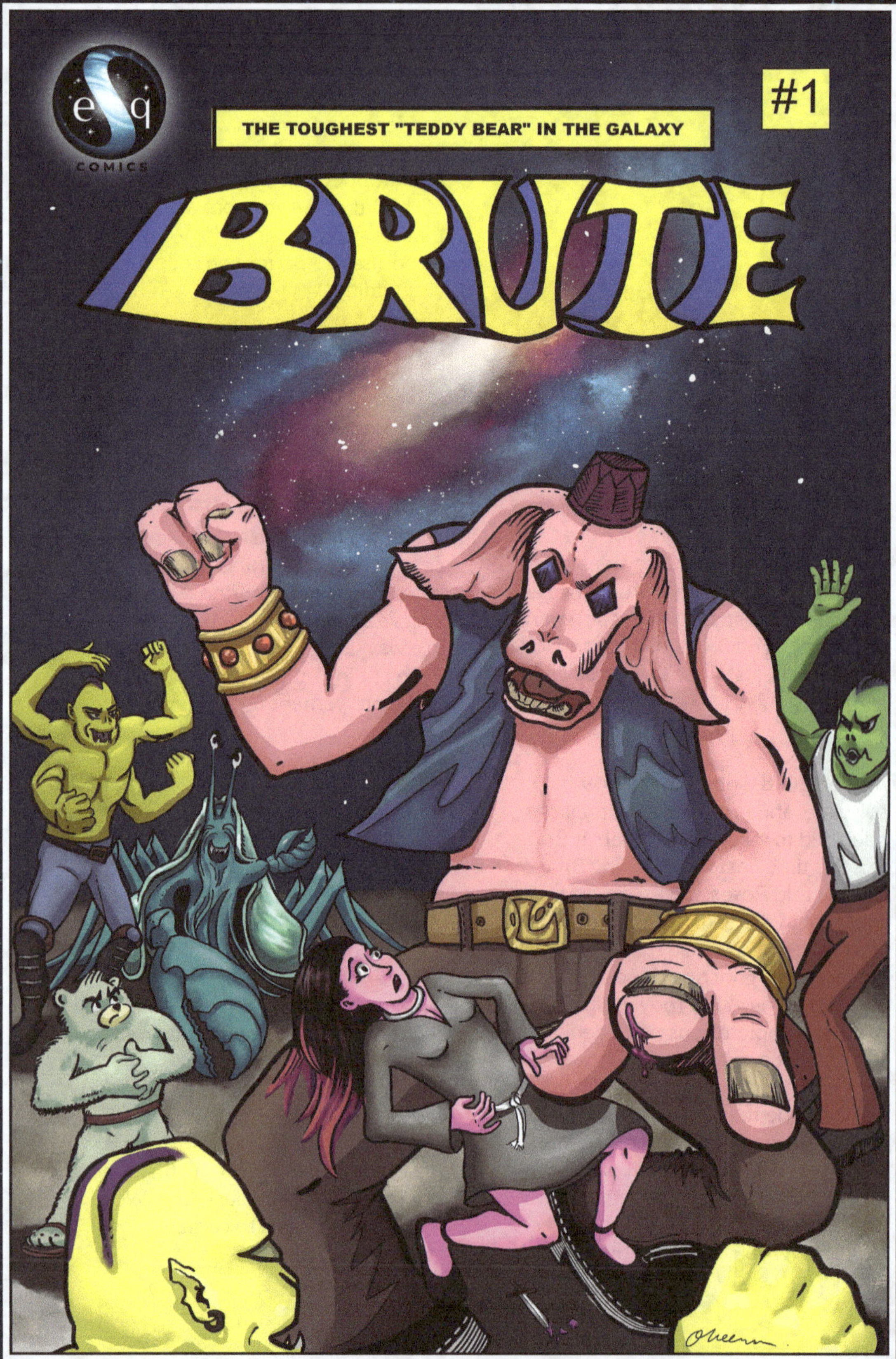

THE TOUGHEST "TEDDY BEAR" IN THE GALAXY

BRUTE

#1

MOOHOOVAN STATION, PERSEUS ARM OF THE MILKY WAY GALAXY....
THIS IS IT, CAESAR! LAST PORT OF CALL BEFORE WE ARRIVE ON EARTH!
WHAT DO YOU THINK IT'LL BE LIKE, CAESAR? IT LOOKS SO PRETTY FROM THE IMAGES. I'M SURE YOU'LL LOVE IT. YOU CAN FINALLY CATCH ALL THOSE CAT THINGS: BIRDS, MICE, SQUIRRAWS, NO, AH... SQUIRLIES? SQUIRTLES?
PRRRRRRRRRR.

MISS KHAN. THE SHIP IS ALMOST READY, WE'LL BE LEAVING SOON.
...AND THEN EARTH, RIGHT? HOW MUCH LONGER WILL IT TAKE?
YES, ABOUT THAT...

YOU SEE MISS KAHN, WE KNOW YOU CAN'T STOMACH OUR FOOD...
I'M SORRY I ATE ALL OF YOUR PRIME FOOD. MY UNCLE WILL REIMBURSE YOU ONCE WE GET TO EARTH.
...I HOPE...

HA, HA, HA... NO WORRIES! IN FACT, WE ALL PUT IN SOME CREDITS SO YOU CAN BUY HUMAN FOOD FOR... THE... AH TRIP.
OH MY GOSH! THANK YOU! YOU DIDN'T HAVE TO DO THAT!
IT WAS THE LEAST WE COULD DO. I'VE SENT THEM YOUR BIO-SCAN.
CLICK

THAT'S SO NICE! HOW DO I GET TO THE MARKET?
JUST TAKE THE TUBE! YOU CAN'T MISS IT! ENJOY!

OKAY! I'LL BE RIGHT BACK! BYE!
NO RUSH! WE'LL BE AWHILE STILL!
SHUNK!
I HATE YOU.

AS SHE STEPS OUT OF THE STATION TRANSPORTATION SYSTEM, ROSE KHAN BEHOLDS THE LARGEST ENVIRONMENT SHE'S EVER SEEN., FILLED WITH HUNDREDS OF BEINGS FROM ACROSS THE GALAXY. MANY RACES SHE MET ON HER HOME STATION, SOME SHE LEARNED ABOUT IN HOME STUDY AND YET OTHERS... SHE NEVER EVEN IMAGINED. RARELY HAS ANY HUMAN BEHELD SUCH A SIGHT, AND NEVER BEFORE ONE AS YOUNG AS 14!
HOLY... THIS PLACE IS IMMENSE! LOOK AT ALL THE STORES AND PEOPLE AND RACES!

WE'RE BACK! THEY HAVE EVERYTHING HERE. I EVEN GOT...
MEE-OOOOW...
WHAT'S THE MATTER, CAESAR?

WHERE'S THE SHIP?

WHERE'S TH... O-OH MY GOD. OH MY GOD! WHAT...?
BEEP!...
...BEEP!

STOP. STOP. THINK IT THROUGH, ROSE! THEY WOULDN'T LEAVE YOU. THEY WOULDN'T...
I MUST BE ON THE WRONG DOCK!

EXCUSE ME! I'M LOOKING FOR THE BOVINESE SHIP 'GRAND LADY'. WHAT DOCK IS IT AT?
YOU'RE ON THE RIGHT DOCK.
THANK GOD! WHERE'S THE SHIP?

THEY LEFT ABOUT AN HOUR AGO.
NO! THEY CAN'T! I'M SUPPOSED TO BE ABOARD THAT SHIP!
I CHECKED THE LOGS, ALL HANDS WERE ABOARD.
I'M NOT CREW! THEY WERE TRANSPORTING ME!

ARE YOU SAYING THEY ABANDONED YOU? THAT'S A CRIMINAL OFFENCE!
RIGHT! W-WHAT DO WE DO?
LET'S SEE YOUR BOARDING PASS...

I... I DON'T HAVE ONE.
YOU DON'T...?
I HAD ONE... FOR A EUFONIAN SHIP THAT WAS GOING TO MY HOMEWORLD. BUT THEY GOT RECALLED. THE CAPTAIN ARRANGED FOR THE BOVINES TO TAKE ME THE REST OF THE WAY.

SIGH FINE. LET'S SEE THE EUFONIAN BOARDING PASS.
IT'S AH... STILL ONBOARD.

LET ME CALL THEM!
...GO AHEAD...
THEY PROBABLY FORGOT! WE CAN GET THIS SORTED OUT!
UM HMM...

BRZZT *BRZZT* *BRZZT*
SOMETHING'S WRONG... THEY'RE NOT PICKING UP!
UMM HMM...

BRZZT *BRZZT* *BRZZT*
OH MY GOD. THEY DITCHED ME.

SOB
W-WHAT AM I GOING TO DO...?
YOU MUST REPORT IT TO STATION SECURITY.
O-OKAY... *SNIFF*

TAKE THE TUBE TO OSSABANIAN STATION AND THEN GO UP, I THINK, 10 LEVELS. IT'LL SAY SECURITY. YOU'LL FIND IT.
THANKS...
YEAH... GOOD LUCK KID.
MEOW.

MOOHOOVAN SECURITY OFFICE - 3 HOURS LATER.
NEXT.

HI. I NEED TO FILE AN ABANDONMENT REPORT.
YOU ARE THE ABANDONED PARTY?
YEAH. CAESAR MY CAT AND I.

BOARDING PASSES...
I DON-- WE DIDN'T HAVE BOARDING PASSES! THEY WERE DOING US A FAVOUR!
SNORT YOU CAN'T FILE WITHOUT THE PROPER PAPERWORK!

B-BUT WHAT AM I SUPPOSED TO DO?
GO HOME.
THAT'S WHERE I WAS HEADED! I'VE NO MONEY TO BOARD PASSAGE ON ANOTHER SHIP - IF ANY ARE EVEN GOING MY WAY!
DO YOU HAVE ANY FAMILY OR FRIENDS YOU CAN CALL? MAYBE THEY CAN SEND SOME CREDITS.
TH-THEY'RE ALL DEAD!
SORRY...

W-WHAT AM I GOING TO DO?
GET A JOB. MAKE CREDITS. GO HOME.
A JOB? I... I DON'T KNOW HOW TO WORK!
SNORT FIGURE IT OUT!

ANYTHING ELSE?
WAIT! YOU CAN'T JUST LEA--

NEXT!
BEAT IT, KID!
BU---

ROSE IS CRUSHED WITH DISILLUSIONMENT AND DIS--APPOINTMENT. NEVER BEFORE HAS AN ADULT REFUSED TO HELP.
EVERYONE SHE'S EVER DEPENDED UPON IS GONE. IS THERE NO-ONE SHE CAN TURN TO?
MEOW!
UNCLE ENRIQUE!

THEY DIDN'T HELP?
NO. BUT MAYBE MY UNCLE CAN PAY FOR TRANSPORT. I'M SORRY, BUT CAN YOU SEE IF ANY SHIPS ARE HEADED FOR EARTH?
DID YOU SAY TO... 'SOIL'?
NO, EA... PLANET 45892736452!

GEEZ KID, THAT'S NOT EVEN ON THE GALACTIC ARM, SOME RARELY TRAVELED OFFSHOOT!
BUT SOMEONE IS GOING THAT WAY?
YEAH, THERE'S A COUPLE INHABITED SYSTEMS... WAIT... NO.

THERE'S A TRAVEL ADVISORY TO NOT GO TO YOUR PLANET... WAR IS IMMINENT! THAT EXPLAINS IT. NO WONDER THEY DUMPED YOU.
W-WAR?

OH MY GOSH! CAN I CALL MY UNCLE?
I DUNNO KID. THAT'S A LOT OF CREDIT!
PLEASE! MAYBE HE CAN SEND MONEY?
OKAY... AS LONG AS HE ACCEPTS THE CHARGES.

Rosita! It's so **good** to see you! Are you **okay**? I'm **so**, so sorry about your family.

Ah... thanks... **uncle**, the **bovines**, they've **stranded** me on a space station. I can't get to **earth**!

Don't worry. Come **join us** and all will be well.

Yes! I want to! Can you **help**?

Of course. We must all help one another.

AS ROSE DEALS WITH HER LAST HOPE EVAPORATING, LET'S TURN OUR ATTENTION TO A DISTANT TIME AND PLACE WHERE LESS SAVORY CHARACTERS ARE ABOUT TO BEGIN THEIR OWN JOURNEY...

WHAT IS IT?
THE TARGET HAS BEEN FOUND!
ARE YOU SURE?
OH YES MASTER! MULTIPLE CONFIRMED SIGHTINGS!
FINALLY! WHERE IS HE?
HE WAS SPOTTED ENTERING HIS BUNKER IN NEW PUMIKA CITY, DOMOKA!
DOMOKA? HMMM.....
HIS BUNKER IS TOO HEAVILY FORTIFIED AND GUARDED BUT IF WE WAIT HIM OUT THEN ---

NO.
NO...?
WE GO NOW.
BUT MASTER! WE CAN'T POSSIBLY---

SHUT-UP, $#!^HEAD! YOU SEE THOSE MISCREANT MERCENARIES? THEY ARE EATING THE LAST OF MY FOOD! IF THEY DON'T GET PAID SOON, IT'LL BE MY HEAD THEY'RE AFTER!
BUT MASTER, SURELY...

TO DOMOKA, NOW!
YES... MASTER.
FINALLY, HE'LL BE MINE. AND WITH HIM... REDEMPTION!

MOOHOOVAN STATION MARKETPLACE.

HOURS LATER...
Yb....

YO! I SAID GET OFF MY BENCH!
W-WHAT?
THIS IS MY BENCH. GET YOUR OWN!
EWWW.....

OH, LET IT STAY. CAN'T YOU SEE IT'S NEWLY CAST-OFF? BESIDES....
HMMPH! WELL, AIN'T IT YOUR LUCKY DAY. ENJOY THE PRIME REAL ESTATE.
T-THANKS...
HISSSSS...

YAWN
MORNING, CAESAR.
...WAIT...
SNIFF, SNIFF...

WHAT THE CRAKIS???
MY FOOD!
WHERE'S MY FOOD?
IT'S GONE!

FOUR HOURS LATER...
NEXT!
THESE GUYS STOLE MY FOOD!

YOU SAW THEM STEAL IT?
NO, I WAS SLEEPING!
SLEEPING? WHERE?
MMM HMMM...
ON A BENCH IN THE MARKET - IT'S ALL THERE!

WHAT'S THIS?
LOITERING INFRACTION. LETTING YOU OFF WITH A WARNING.
WHAT ABOUT MY FOOD?
ANYONE COULD HAVE TAKEN THAT.
NEXT!

NO! UNACCEPTABLE!
MY SHIP'S GONE! MY FOOD'S GONE! YOU'RE SUPPOSED TO HELP ME! WHAT AM I TO DO?
STOP BEING A VICTIM. NOW GET OUT, BEFORE I HAVE YOU THROWN OUT!

LATER ON, OUTSIDE THE SECURITY OFFICE.
WHAT AM I GOING TO DO, CAESAR? I WISH MY MOM AND DAD WERE HERE. THEY'D KNOW WHAT TO DO.
"GET A JOB! STOP BEING A VICTIM!"
HUH, THOSE EGGHEADS WOULD PROBABLY STUDY THEIR WAY OUT OF... WAIT! THAT'S IT! COME ON, LET'S FIND A LIBRARY!

ONE HOUR LATER AT MOOHOOVAN STATION LIBRARY...
...MEASURE THE GIN AND VERMOUTH INTO A MIXING GLASS...
"MEASURE THE..." HEY! STOP IT, CAESAR!
MEE-OOWW!

THREE HOURS LATER AT MOOHOOVAN STATION LIBRARY...
CAESAR! STOP IT! WHAT'S THE MATTER WITH YOU?
MEE-OOW!!

CLOSING TIME FOR THE LIBRARY...
DANG IT CAESEAR! WOULD YOU STOP!!
MEOW!

I'M SORRY. I KNOW YOU'RE JUST HUNGRY. ME TOO.
MEE-OW.
...WE HAVE NO FOOD.

THE NEXT MORNING...
EEWK!
CRUNCH CRUNCH

YAWN
WHAT IS THAT...
CRUNCH CRUNCH
OH. GROSS.

WELL AT LEAST YOU'RE EATING. I'M STARVING...
CRUNCH CRACK GULP

STOP! THIEF! SOMEONE STOP HER!
I'VE GOT HER!

WHAT DO YOU WANT ME TO DO WITH HER?
HOLD THE THIEF FOR SECURITY!

TWO HOURS LATER...
I FILED A REPORT BUT YOU GUYS DID NOTHING. SO I'M STUCK HERE. NO BED, NO FOOD, NO CREDITS (THANKS FOR THE SANDWICH, BY THE WAY). I DIDN'T KNOW WHAT TO DO. I TRIED MY UNCLE ON EARTH BUT HE'S JOINED SOME KIND OF CULT. SAY... AREN'T YOU FROM EARTH?

NEVER BEEN THERE.
BUT AREN'T YOU A DOLPHIN? FROM EARTH? DO YOU KNOW WHAT'S HAPPENING THERE?
FIRST OFF, WE CALL IT "WATER". SECONDLY, YOU HUMANS HAVE MADE SUCH A MESS OF IT, I STOPPED PAYING ATTENTION.

WAIT - YOU'RE A HUMAN?
Y-YES.
EVERYONE! STOP WHAT YOU'RE DOING! YOU CAN ALL GO HOME!

HA HA HA!
HA HA! HA
WE HAVE A HUMAN HERE! THE GALAXY IS SAVED!
HA HA
HA HA

HA
HA
SORRY. COULDN'T RESIST.
YEAH, I BET.
YOU'RE SO BAD.
HA
HA

23

SERIOUSLY, ISN'T THERE ANYTHING YOU CAN DO TO HELP? TOSS ME IN JAIL? AT LEAST I'LL GET FED.
HONEY, YOU DON'T WANT TO BE IN THERE! THEY'LL TEAR YOU APART!
YOU WOULDN'T LAST A DAY.

LOOK KID, WE CAN SHOW YOU WHERE YOU CAN GET FED. IT'S NOT NICE BUT--- JOY... WHAT ARE YOU THINKING?
WE CAN'T JUST LEAVE HER.

YOU'RE SUCH A BLEEDING-HEART, JOY. WHAT ARE YOU GOING TO DO? ADOPT HER?
NO. BUT SHE IS MY FELLOW WATERLING.
OH PLEASE, ANYTHING YOU CAN DO!

SO? WHAT'S THE PLAN THEN?
JARVEET.
HA HA HA! HE'S GOING TO LOVE THIS!

SGT. JOY! WHAT A PLEASURE. WOULD YOU LIKE THE USUAL?
NO THANKS JARVEET. HERE ON BUSINESS. I'D LIKE YOU TO MEET ROSE AND CAESAR.
WELCOME TO MY DINER!

SO WHAT SORT OF BUSINESS?
I NEED YOU TO GIVE THEM WORK, ROOM AND BOARD.
THIS ISN'T A SOUP KITCHEN AND I DON'T NEED THE HELP.
SEEMS TO ME YOU OWE ME ONE.
AND YOU'RE GOING TO WASTE THAT ON THESE TWO? A HUMAN AND A FURBAG?
INDULGE ME.
SIGH ...FINE. ANYTHING FOR YOU, JOY.

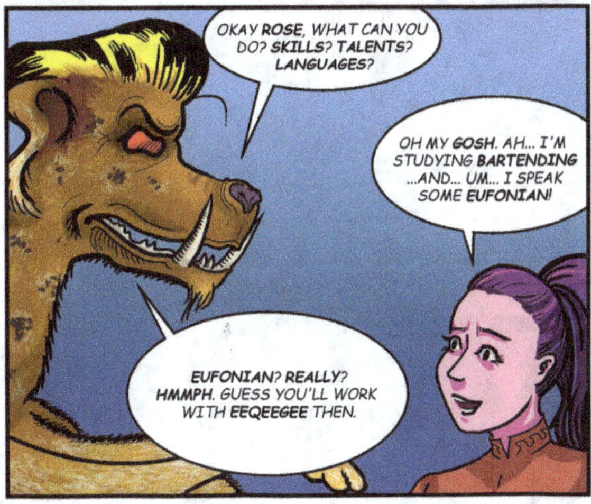

OKAY ROSE, WHAT CAN YOU DO? SKILLS? TALENTS? LANGUAGES?
OH MY GOSH. AH... I'M STUDYING BARTENDING ...AND... UM... I SPEAK SOME EUFONIAN!
EUFONIAN? REALLY? HMMPH. GUESS YOU'LL WORK WITH EEQEEGEE THEN.

AND WHAT ABOUT YOU? ANY SKILLS?
CHUCKLE HE DOESN'T SPEAK.
WHY NOT?
HE'S MY PET. HE'S... JUST COMPANY. HE CAN'T DO ANYTHI---

DID HE JUST CATCH A REAWK???
EEK!! A REAWK!!
YEAH... AH... I'M SORRY, HE'S REALLY HUN---
THAT'S INCREDIBLE! THOSE DANG THINGS OUTSMART MY DROIDS ALL THE TIME! CAESAR, YOU'RE HIRED!
...AT LEAST ONE OF YOU ARE USEFUL...

A NEW LIFE BEGINS. AS ROUTINE SETS IN, HOURS QUICKLY FADE TO DAYS. DAYS BECOME WEEKS.
WHEN SHE'S NOT WORKING, SHE'S STUDYING.
...TRAINING HER MIND AND BODY TO BE PREPARED AND BE READY FOR THIS NEW LIFE.

MONTHS FLOW INTO YEARS AND ROSE BECOMES EVER MORE INDEPEDENT, MOVING OUT FROM THE DINER...
ABLE TO TAKE CARE OF HERSELF...
WHAM
NO LONGER A VICTIM OF LIFE OR CIRCUMSTANCE.

COSMIC STORM.
THANKS ROSE.
OH LOOK LINNI, NEW GIRL!

YOU LIKE HER, LINNI?
SHE'S A PRETTY COLOUR. LINNI LIKE.
GO SIT IN THE BACK. YOU'LL SCARE HER. I'LL TALK TO HER. OKAY?
OKAY.

LAVA PIT. STEAMING, PLEASE.
SURE THING.
NEVER SEEN A HUMAN THIS FAR OUT BEFORE. HOW'D YOU GET HERE?

MY PARENTS WERE SCIENTISTS ON AN INTERGALACTIC RESEARCH STATION ON THE EDGE OF THE GALAXY, WHERE I WAS BORN. WHEN I TURNED 14 THEY DECIDED TO SEND ME HOME TO EARTH VIA AN EUFONIAN SHIP. BUT A MONTH AFTER WE LEFT, THE STATION WAS ATTACKED BY PIRATES AND... DESTROYED. THE EUFONIANS RECALLED THEIR SHIP, SO THE CAPTAIN ARRANGED PASSAGE ABOARD A BOVINESE SHIP, BUT THEY JUST DUMPED ME HERE.

THAT'S PERFECT! -LY, UH, TERRIBLE! SO YOU'RE JUST STRANDED HERE?
FOR FOUR YEARS NOW.
WOW. Y'KNOW, I'M HEADING TO EARTH. YOU'D BE WELCOME TO COME ALONG.
Y-YOU'D TAKE ME?
WHY NOT?
BUT YOU CAN'T TELL ANYONE, 'CAUSE WHAT I'M TRADING WITH HUMANS AIN'T EXACTLY LEGAL.
HEY, NO PROBLEM. I'VE NO ONE TO TELL ANYWAY.

WE'RE HERE!
GOOD TIMING. LINNI, HELP HER WITH HER BAGS.
HI LINNI! AND THIS IS CAESAR.

THANKS AGAIN. I CAN'T BELIEVE YOU'RE DOING THIS! WOW... LOOK AT THIS PLACE IT'S SO BIG!
PLACTORI CREW...

WHAT DID YOU TELL PEOPLE?
DON'T WORRY. JUST THAT I WAS HITCHING A RIDE TO EARTH. NO DETAILS. AND I DON'T EXPECT A FREE RIDE. I'M WILLING TO WORK.
GOOD.

NOW, LINNI.
CLICK
W-WHA...?
IT'S A SLAVE COLLAR. TRY TO LEAVE, REMOVE IT OR HURT ME AND IT'LL LIQUIFY YOUR BRAINS.

YOU CRAKIS!! I'LL---
ARRRGH!!

TOLD YOU.
LINNI, PUT HER - AND THIS FURBAG - IN HER ROOM.
YES, JORJ.
NNNOOOO.... WHY?

FOUR YEARS LATER...

UGH. WHY DIDN'T I PAY MORE ATTENTION IN EUFONIAN WRITING CLASS? I THINK IF I CUT THIS WIRE... OH CAESAR IF I'M WRONG... HERE GOES...
SNIP

ARRIVAL AT TARS STATION IN 4 HOURS.
CAN I COME ALONG THIS TIME?
YOU KNOW YOU CAN'T GO OFF-SHIP.
YOU TOOK ME OFF TO HAVE THE SHIP FUMIGATED... YOU CAN DO IT AGAIN.

THINK OF HOW HANDY IT'LL BE TO HAVE ME WITH YOU ALL THE TIME... TO SEE ABOUT YOUR EVERY WHIM.
I CAN GO ALL KINDS OF PLACES PLACTORIS CAN'T.
AND NOT MESS UP YOUR ORDERS!
HMMM...

DID YOU HAVE TO BRING CAESAR?

HE HASN'T BEEN OFF-SHIP EITHER. HE WON'T BE ANY TROUBLE.
VEEEZZT!

30

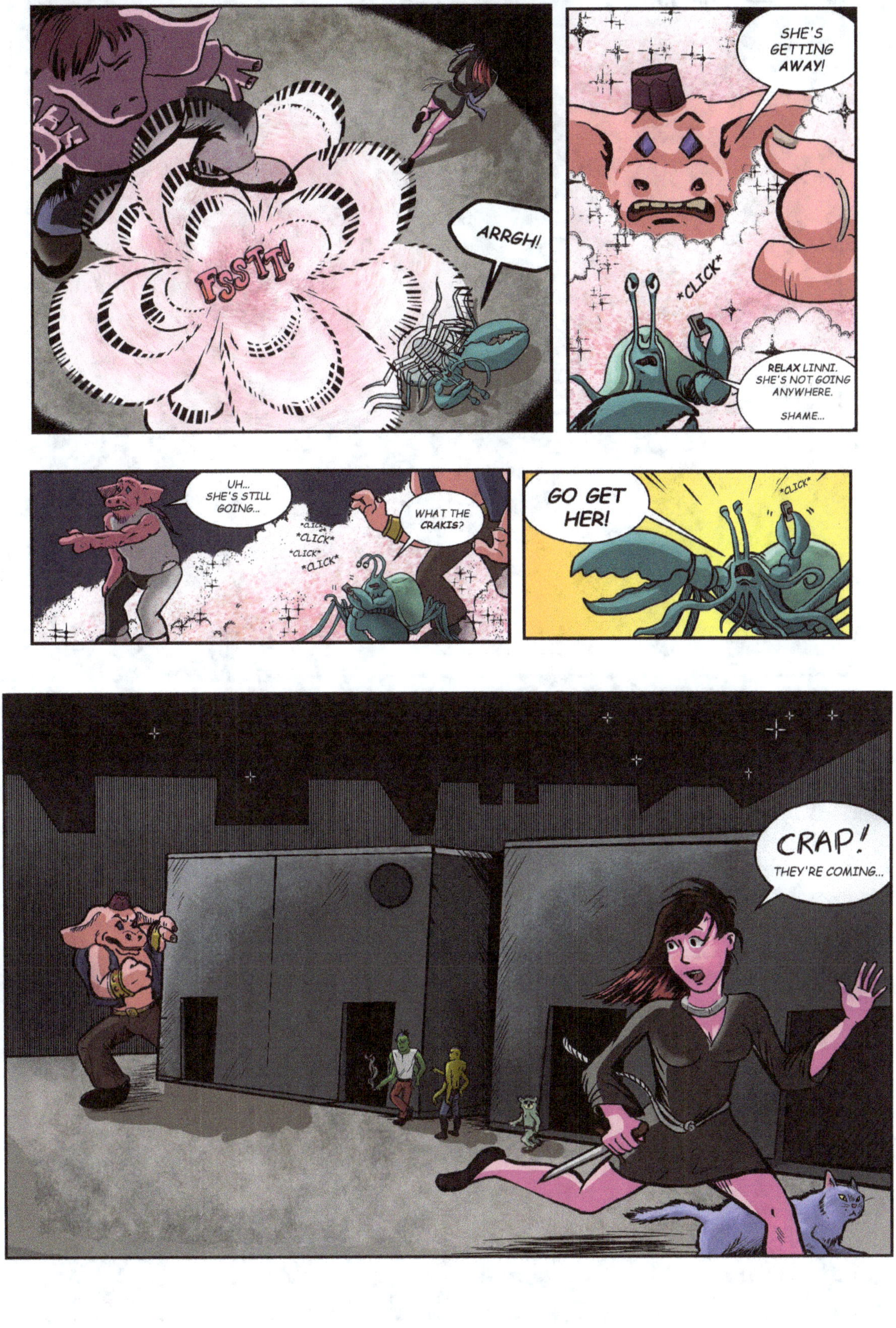

ARRGH!
FSSTT!

SHE'S GETTING AWAY!
CLICK
RELAX LINNI. SHE'S NOT GOING ANYWHERE.
SHAME...

UH... SHE'S STILL GOING...
CLICK
CLICK
CLICK
WHAT THE CRAKIS?

GO GET HER!
CLICK

CRAP!
THEY'RE COMING...

HELP!
SOMEONE HELP!
I'M BEING HELD HOSTAGE!

HA HA!
NO-ONE WILL HELP YOU HERE, ROSE!
RUN, CAESAR!

HOLD STILL!
OUCH!

THAT HURT!
GUH...
OH OH...
ZZZAP!

AAACK!
GONG
YOU HURT LINNI!

GOT YOU!
AGH!

UHHH!
NNNNNN.....
KRFESSH!
HANDS OFF THE LADY!

CRACK!

--IGHT?
SORRY ABOUT THE FALL.
I COULDN'T CATC--

--TORI GOONS ARE OUT...
BUT WE CAN'T STAY HERE.
W-WHO?

SORRY, WHERE ARE
MY MANNERS? MY NAME
IS KODEE BUT EVERYONE
CALLS ME---

BRUTE

eSq COMICS
THE TOUGHEST "TEDDY BEAR" IN THE GALAXY
#2
BRUTE

"SO HERE I AM, PLAYING HERO ON THIS ESSENCE-FORSAKEN ROCK ON THE OUTSKIRTS OF THE MILKY WAY."

"I'VE NO IDEA WHO - OR EVEN WHAT - I'D JUST SAVED, EXCEPT HER NAME (I THINK IT'S A HER) IS ROSE AND SHE'S GOT A SLAVE COLLAR AROUND HER NECK."

MY NAME IS KODEE BUT EVERYONE CALLS ME...
BRUTE

"WHEN I'D ARRIVED, SHE WAS TRYING TO FIGHT OFF 3 - COUNT 'EM - 3 PLACTORIS. THAT'S RIGHT, THE LARGEST OF ALL BIPEDS IN THE GALAXY AND THIS SCRAWNY GIRL THINKS SHE CAN FIGHT OFF 3 OF THEM, ALONE. SHE LASTED A WHOLE DOZEN MORE SECONDS THAN I'D GIVEN HER CREDIT FOR AND WOULD HAVE MADE HER MAMA PROUD (IF HER MAMA CONDONED VIOLENCE)."

"PROBLEM IS, SHE'S A SLAVE. SHE BELONGS TO SOME--ONE, AND IT'S NOT THESE SLOW-WITTED PLACTORIS THAT OWN HER. NO, IT'S MOST LIKELY A CRABI THAT OWNS THE LOT OF THEM...
...AND HE'S GONNA WANT HIS PROPERTY BACK."

AH... WE SHOULD GO.
NNNNN....
B-BRUTE...?

WAIT... YOU DID THIS?
YEAH... WELL, I HAD THE ELEMENT OF SURPRISE AND YOU'D AL-READY SOFTENED THEM UP BUT... YEAH.

NNNNNN...
BUT... HOW? ANYWAY, THANKS FO---
NO TIME FOR THAT.

HEY! WHAT THE HECK ARE YOU---
GETTING US OUT OF HERE.

WHAAAAAAAAHH!
HHSSSST!
NNNN... ROSE? ROSE! THAT'S LINNI'S ROSE!

SOME TIME LATER...
BOUNCE!
WHUMP!

PLEASE! JUST... PUT ME DOWN!
WE'RE HERE.

THIS IS YOUR PLACE? IT'S LOVELY.
IT'S MY LANDLORD'S. I JUST RENT THE BASEMENT APART-MENT.
MMMRRRRROOOWWW

YOU'D BETTER COME IN---
CAESAR! NO!!
MEEERRRWW

CAESAR, GET OUT HERE!
WOULD YOU HUSH? THEY'LL HEAR YOU! CAESAR HAS THE RIGHT IDEA; YOU DON'T WANT TO BE OUTSIDE WHEN THEY COME LOOKING!

WHY ARE YOU HELPING ME? WHAT DO YOU WANT?
WHY AM I...? HOW ABOUT "THANKS FOR SAVING MY LIFE, MR. BRUTE SIR - YOU'RE AWESOME!" SERIOUSLY? GET IN - OR DON'T - NOT MY PROBLEM. BUT THOSE PLACTORIS OUT THERE ARE YOUR PROBLEM!

"WHY AM I...?" WHY DO I EVEN BOTHER? THERE'S NO GRATITUDE FROM ANYONE HERE ON TARS STATION! WHY'D I THINK SHE'D BE ANY DIFFERENT?
WAIT! ...I... I'M COMING. I'M SORRY.

CAESAR! ARE YOU---
HE'S FINE. THERE'S TONS OF ROOM. THIS PLACE IS WAY TOO BIG FOR ME.
...TOO BIG?

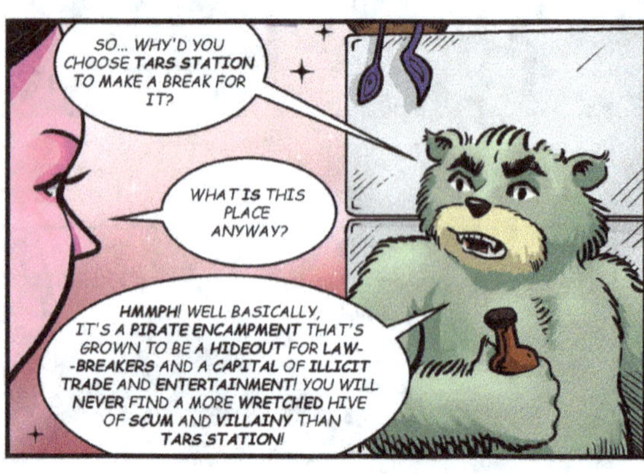

SO... WHY'D YOU CHOOSE TARS STATION TO MAKE A BREAK FOR IT?
WHAT IS THIS PLACE ANYWAY?
HMMPH! WELL BASICALLY, IT'S A PIRATE ENCAMPMENT THAT'S GROWN TO BE A HIDEOUT FOR LAW-BREAKERS AND A CAPITAL OF ILLICIT TRADE AND ENTERTAINMENT! YOU WILL NEVER FIND A MORE WRETCHED HIVE OF SCUM AND VILLAINY THAN TARS STATION!

"HIVE OF SCUM?"
YEAH I DON'T KNOW WHY I SAID THAT...

WHY DON'T THE AUTHORITIES SHUT IT DOWN?
HA! THIS IS DEEP SPACE. THERE'S NO COPS WITHIN 40 PARSECS OF HERE.
OH... HOW DO I... LEAVE?
I'VE BEEN WANTING TO DO THAT MYSELF. YOU NEED A RIDE. AND THEY'LL WANT CREDITS - PLENTY OF THEM. OR... THEY MIGHT JUST TAKE ALL YOUR CREDITS AND SHOOT YOU INTO SPACE. RISKY AFFAIR, THAT.

THEY'D DO THAT... ?
P-I-I-I-RATES...
LOOK, YOU'RE WELCOME TO STAY. THERE'S LOTS OF ROOM AND I DOUBT THEY'LL EVER FIND YOU HERE.

WHAT ARE YOU ANYWAY? NEVER SEEN YOUR KIND BEFORE.
I'M A HUMAN.
HUU-MEN? FROM THE PLANET HUME?

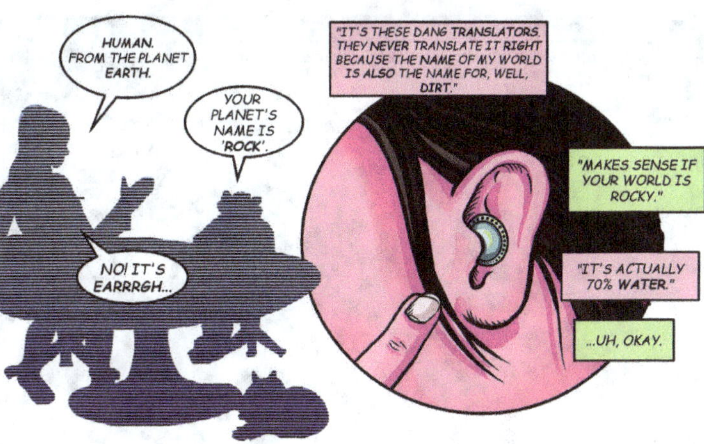

HUMAN. FROM THE PLANET EARTH.
YOUR PLANET'S NAME IS 'ROCK'.
NO! IT'S EARRRGH...
"IT'S THESE DANG TRANSLATORS, THEY NEVER TRANSLATE IT RIGHT BECAUSE THE NAME OF MY WORLD IS ALSO THE NAME FOR, WELL, DIRT."
"MAKES SENSE IF YOUR WORLD IS ROCKY."
"IT'S ACTUALLY 70% WATER."
...UH, OKAY.

AND YOU? I'VE NEVER SEEN YOUR KIND EITHER.
I KNOW WHO YOU ARE... BUT WHAT SPECIES ARE YOU?
I'M... BRUTE.
I'M... A... PERSON.
CHUCKLE YES BRUTE... BUT WHAT KIND?
THE... GOOD KIND?

WHAT'S YOUR HOME WORLD?
...
THE PLANET YOU'RE FROM... WHAT'S IT CALLED?
IT DOESN'T HAVE A NAME.
IT DOESN'T HAVE A--- BY THE ESSENCE! YOU'RE A PRIMITIVE!

YOUR PEOPLE, THEY'RE NOT SPACE-FARING?
NO. WE'RE... I HEARD IT CALLED: IRON-AGED.
SO... HOW DID YOU END UP HERE?

IT'S A LONG STORY...
I'VE LITERALLY NOWHERE TO GO!
RIGHT. OKAY THEN...

"IMAGINE A PLACE WITH THE NICEST, GENTLEST, MOST CARING PEOPLE YOU COULD EVER HOPE TO MEET. THAT'D DESCRIBE EVERY--ONE THERE - EXCEPT FOR ME AND MY PA. LIKE MY PA, I WAS THE BIGGEST, MOST ORNERY CUSS AROUND - AND AN ICE MINER."
"ICE MINER?"
"BACK HOME, WATER ONLY EXISTED AS ICE AND AL--MOST ALL OF IT UNDERGROUND. BUT THIS MINE WAS STRANGE. IT DIDN'T HAVE MUCH ICE - JUST USELESS GOLD. LOTS AND LOTS OF GOLD."
CREAK!
MOVE!
KESTER!

THANKS, KODEE!
YOU'S ALMOS' A SMEAR ON DA GROUND!
GEE, THANKS JAWKINS.
THUDD!

ARE YOU HURT?
LEG'S BANGED UP. DON'T THINK IT'S BROKEN.
BUT DANG THIS GOLD! WHAT THE HECK ARE WE DOING HERE? IT'S JUST GOLD, GOLD, GOLD THAT WE'RE DIGGING UP AND SHIPPING OUT, BUT TO WHERE? GOLD AIN'T NO GOOD TO NO-ONE!
"WHAT'S WRONG WITH GOLD?"
"IT'S VERY COMMON. WORTHLESS. TOO SOFT A METAL TO MAKE ANY--THING WORTHWHILE. IT JUST FLATTENS INTO A POOL."

WHO CARES? WE'RE GETTING PAID.
PAID? FOR WHAT? WITH WHAT? THEY DON'T MAKE MONEY SELLING GOLD! THEY NEED ICE, OR AT LEAST IRON FOR THAT! ALL WE EVER SEEM TO MINE IS GOLD! SOMETHING'S NOT RIGHT!
MAMA SAYS "JAWKINS' DON'T GO ASKIN' MANY QUEST--IONS. YOU'S JUS' GIT YOU'SELF IN TROUBLE!"
YOU LISTEN TO YOUR MAMA!

YOU'D DO WELL TO LISTEN TO JAWKINS' MAMA TOO, KESTER!
COZ, DON'T YOU CARE THAT THEY AREN'T TELLING US THE TRUTH? DON'T YOU WANT TO KNOW WHAT'S GOING ON? I DO! NEXT DAY OFF, I'M FOLLOWING THAT SHIPMENT - I'M GOING TO SEE WHERE IT GOES!
DON'T YOU DARE. AND NO, I DON'T CARE. THE ONLY THING I CARE ABOUT RIGHT NOW IS MY WEDDING DAY!

A WEEK LATER...
ABOUT TIME YOU DID SOMETHING USEFUL WITH YOUR LIFE, BOY! I THOUGHT YOU'D BE MOOCHING OFF ME FOR THE REST OF MY DAYS!
DON'T MIND HIM. RELAX; YOU'RE ABOUT TO MARRY THE MOST WONDERFUL GIRL IN TOWN. THIS IS NO TIME TO LOSE YOUR TEMPER.
WHY I OUGHTA...
YEAH.... YEAH, YOU'RE RIGHT. THANKS, COUSIN.
...

...AND THERE SHE IS!
OH WOW!
WELL DONE, BOY!
SHEE-OOT! I'D SURE LIKE TO GIVE HER SOME FINE LOVIN'!

WHAT THE...
NO.... NO!
SHE'S WAY TOO GOOD FOR YOU!

WHY YOU LITTLE...

GASP!
YOU'RE RUINING MY WEDDING!
SMACK

TIMEESHA!...

TIMEESHA!!
NICE ONE, JERK!

SHORTLY...
HERE YOU ARE! TIMEESHA I'M...I'M... SOR... IT'S JAWKINS FAULT! PLEASE! COME BACK, BABY! I LOVE YOU! I'LL... I'LL MAKE IT UP TO YOU BABE! COME BACK, EVERYONE'S WAITING!
NO.

BABY...I...PLEASE! YOU MAKE ME WANT TO BE A BETTER PERSON. I'VE BEEN GOOD. I HAVEN'T LOST MY TEMPER IN MONTHS!
I CAN'T HON... I CAN'T! YOU'RE JUST A... A...

A... BRUTE!

AH DITCH THIS... I DON'T NEED YOU. I DON'T NEED ANYONE!
"SO I LEFT. I'M TOLD SHE CRIED FOR DAYS AFTERWARDS. BUT I NEVER SAW HER AGAIN..."

LATER THAT WEEK...
I CAN'T BELIEVE THIS IS HOW YOU'RE SPENDING YOUR DAY OFF.
KEEPING YOU OUT OF TROUBLE. WHAT'S THE PLAN?
THAT'S A STUPID PLAN.
YOU GOT A BETTER ONE?
KODEE, WHAT ARE YOU DOING HERE? I THOUGHT YOU DIDN'T CARE.
AS SOON AS THE GUARDS AREN'T LOOKING, I'LL JUMP INTO A CART AND BURY MYSELF. THEN I'LL SEE WHERE THIS GOLD REALLY GOES.

YEAH. I GO IN YOUR PLACE. YOU HAVE A WIFE AND KIDS THAT NEED YOU, COZ.
KONK!

NO-ONE NEEDS ME AROUND ANYWAY.
ZZZZZ...

HOURS LATER.
WHERE THE HECK ARE WE?
THERE'S NO-ONE DRIVING THIS TRAIN! AND WHAT THE HECK IS THAT?

VOOOSH!
WHAAAAHH!

WHOOSH!

GOOD JOB, SHIPWRECK! CAN YOU TELL WHAT THEY ONBOARDED?
YES, MASTER. IT APPEARS TO BE SEDIMENT WITH A VERY HIGH CONCENTRATION OF MANY HEAVY EL--EMENTS -- PREDOMINATELY GOLD.
SO THEY'RE MINING SOME UNCHARTED WORLD? THAT'S NOT A CRIME... WHY ALL THE SUBTERFUGE?

MASTER, I AM ABOARD THE VESSEL.

WHAT IS THAT?
IT APPEARS TO BE A DOMESTIC LIFE--FORM, INADVERTENTLY BROUGHT ABOARD WITH THE ORE.
DOMESTIC? YOU TOLD ME THERE WAS NO POSSIBLE WAY ADVANCED LIFE COULD EXIST UNDER SUCH HIGH GRAVITY!
GASP
THAT IS CORRECT. IT IS NOT POSSIBLE.
AND YET... THERE IT IS!
IT DOES NOT COMPUTE.

WHAT'S IT DOING?
I CALCULATE THAT IT IS ATTEMPT--ING TO... SPEAK WITH ME.
GIVE IT A TRANSLATOR!
YES, MASTER... BUT IT WILL NOT WORK. IT WOULD HAVE TO SPEAK A KNOWN LANGUAGE AND I ASSURE YOU... IT IS NOT.

I THOUGHT THOSE THINGS COULD LEARN LANGUAGES?
AFFIRMATIVE, BUT IT TAKES SOME TIME AND HAS TO BE AT LEAST A 71.52% MATCH TO A KNOWN LANG...
UM...IT APPEARS TO WORK FINE.
IT SPEAKS! IT'S INTELLIGENT! DO YOU KNOW WHAT THIS MEANS?

WHAT'S HAPPENING NOW?
THEY ARE DECOMPRESSING THE BAY. IT IS SUFFOCATING.
DO YOU HAVE A PAEG?*
AFFIRMATIVE.
GIVE IT TO HIM!
IT IS AGAINST GALAC-TIC REGULATIONS TO—
JSSSSSSHHHH
SHUT-UP SHIPWRECK AND GIVE IT TO HIM! I NEED HIM ALIVE!
*PAEG - PERSONAL ARTIFICIAL ENVIRONMENT GENERATOR.

RECORDING THAT I AM BEING FORCED TO COMMIT A GALACTIC OFFENSE UNDER DIRECT COMMAND FROM CAPTAIN JERRREECKO KR---
JUST DO IT, SHIPWRECK!
DONE, MASTER.

ASK IT WHAT IT IS.
WHAT ARE YOU?
GASP ...I CAN BREATHE AGAIN... ...THANK YOU... *WHEEZE*

I'M... I AM A... ...A BRUTE.
DON'T THINK THAT'S TRANSLATING RIGHT. IT SAYS IT'S A BRUTE?

CONFIRM IT'S NATIVE.
YOU ARE NATIVE TO THE WORLD THIS ORE IS FROM?
NATIVE TO WHAT? THIS GOLD IS FROM MY MINE.

MASTER, THE BAY LIGHTS HAVE BEEN ACTIVATED.
WHAT THE...?
HIDE! AND HIDE HIM WITH YOU!

WELL, WHAT DO WE HAVE HERE? STOWAWAYS! TELL THE CAPTAIN THE SENSORS WERE RIGHT.
...IT'S TOO LATE, MASTER.
GIANTS...!
CRAKIS.

...AND SO WE WERE CAUGHT BY... HUH?
UH... SPEAKING OF BEING CAUGHT!

IT'S OKAY! GO FIND SOME COVER!
RREEOW!

RRREEOOOWWW!

RRREEOOW!!!
ROSE? LINNI HEARS ROSE'S CAT!

THAT'S IT! BLAST THEIR BACKSIDES!
ROSE? YOU NO ROSE...
ZAP!
ZAP!
WHAT THE CRAKIS?

ROSE?...

GET OFF MY PROPERTY!

LINNI LOOKING FOR ROSE.
WHATEVER THAT IS, THERE'S NONE HERE. GET LOST!

LINNI HEARD CAT IN HERE.
I DON'T CARE WHAT YOU HEARD. GET OFF---
OH GREAT, NOW THERE ARE MORE OF YOU.

WE DON'T MEAN YOU HARM. JUST GIVE US THE HUMAN.
YOU HAVE 3 SECONDS TO GET OFF MY PROPERTY OR YOU WILL ALL BE IN A WORLD OF HURT. 1... 2...

...3!
ZAP!
AAARRGH!
RUN!!

HA HA HA!
IS IT SAFE?

...THESE FRIENDS OF YOURS?
NO. ROSE, MEET GREEN-ORANGE-BLUE-BEIGE-YELLOW, MY LANDLORD. GOBBY, MEET ROSE.
HI.
AH. YOU ARE THE HUMAN THEY ARE LOOKING FOR. NEVER MET A HUMAN BEFORE. WELCOME TO MY PLACE, ROSE.

ANOTHER STRAY, BRUTE? WHAT HAVE I TOLD YOU?
YEAH, I KNOW: "ANYONE ON TARS IS HERE FOR A REASON; THEY'RE TROUBLE." BUT SHE'S NOT FROM TARS. SHE'S AN ESCAPED SLAVE.
YEAH, I SAW THE SLAVE COLLAR. HOW DID YOU ESCAPE?

I FOUND A WAY TO DE-ACTIVATE MY COLLAR.
CLEVER, CARBON-BASED. NOW HOLD STILL WHILE I CUT IT OFF.
OH! THANK YOU!
FLLZZZ!

AN ESCAPED SLAVE IS STILL GOING TO BE TROUBLE.
I KNOW. HER OWNER WILL COME LOOKING FOR HER. I'LL TAKE CARE OF IT IF THEY DO.
OH? LIKE YOU JUST TOOK CARE OF THOSE PLACTORIS?
HE'D KNOCKED THEM ALL OUT, EARLIER.
SORRY I MISSED THAT.

I HOPE YOU HAVE A BETTER PLAN THAN HIDING IN MY BASEMENT. WHAT WERE YOU TWO DISCUSSING BEFORE THIS INTERRUPTION?
BRUTE WAS TELLING ME HOW HE GOT HERE.
HAS HE GOTTEN TO THE PART WHERE THE STUPID PORCUPINIAN DOES HIS 'BRILLIANT' PLAN?
JUST GETTING TO THAT.
OH! WELL THEN PLEASE DO GO ON; I LOVE THIS PART.

WHY IS HE BOUNCING LIKE THAT?
IT APPEARS THE PAEG CANNOT REPLICATE HIS NATURAL GRAVITY, SO HE IS AT THEIR NATIVE GRAVITY.
BUT THESE ARE MCMACAZORKIANS! THEIR GRAVITY IS 3 TIMES THE GALACTIC MEDIAN! AND HE'S STILL BOUNCING LIKE IT'S NOTHING?
AFFIRMATIVE. HIS NATURAL GRA-VITY IS MORE THAN DOUBLE THEIRS.

OKAY SHIPWRECK, LET'S SEE IF THAT McMAC PASSCODE IS WORTH THE MONEY I PAID... TRY HACKING INTO THEIR SYSTEM.
COPY THAT. ATTEMPTING NOW... SHIP'S SENSORS ACCESSED.
ALRIGHT! YOU KNOW WHAT TO DO. STRETCH, ARE THE HOLOGRAMS READY?
AS READY AS THEY'LL EVER BE!

WITH ALL DUE RESPECT CAPTAIN... MCMACS ARE NOT PRONE TO GIVING UP EASILY --- AND THEY HAVE US OUTGUNNED.
RELAX, RED. THIS IS A FRIGATE. THEY WON'T RESIST IF THEY THINK THEY ARE UP AGAINST AN ARMADA OF FIGHTERS.
THIS HAD BETTER WORK...
STRETCH, SHIPWRECK... ON MY MARK - NOW!

EXCELLENT. NOW--- WHAT IN THE ESSENCE?
"ATTENTION MCMACAZORKIAN FRIGATE! THIS IS CAPTAIN JERRREECKO OF THE VANGUARD OF THE GALACTIC FEDERATION. YOU ARE UNDER ARREST FOR UNLAWFUL CONTACT WITH A PRIMITIVE WORLD!"
"IMMEDIATELY DROP YOUR SHIELDS AND PREPARE TO BE BOARDED, OR WE WILL OPEN FIRE!"
CAPTAIN?
CAPTAIN, HERE ARE THE PRISONERS.
DO IT.

SHORTLY...
THEY DON'T LOOK FEDERATION.

BUTCH, LOCK THEIR CONSOLES.
CAPTAIN, ORDER THE SHIP'S COMPUTER TO GIVE ME FULL ACCESS OF ALL CONTROLS.
SHIP, THIS IS CAPTAIN KARLSBURK. TRANSFER ALL AUTHORIZATIONS TO---

CAPTAIN! THERE'S SOMETHING GOING ON WITH THE FEDERATION SHIPS!

MEANWHILE, BACK ONBOARD 'THE VANGUARD'...
WHAT'S HAPPENING???
WE DON'T HAVE ENOUGH POWER TO MAINTAIN THIS MANY HOLOGRAMS!
BUT WE TESTED IT!
NOT WITH ALL WEAPONS AND SHIELDS ONLINE...
KNEW IT! TAKING EVASIVE ACTION.

SHIELDS UP! OPEN FIRE! DETAIN THESE IDIOTS AND TAKE THE LOT OF THEM TO THE AIRLOCK.
ZZARKK!!!

HEY 'BRUTE'-
DO YOU MIND?
I'M WALKING
HERE!
SORRY,
I CAN'T HELP
IT!
THEY CALL
THE PUNY ONE "BRUTE"!
HA HA HA!

HA
HA
HA
HA
THAT
TEARS IT!

THUK!

EAT
QUILLS!
AARGH!

GET
OFF!
GRRROWR
---GAK---
"GAG"

THUD!
POW!

H-HOW DID I DO THAT?
APPARENTLY, IN COMPARISON TO EVERYONE ELSE, YOU ARE INCREDIBLY STRONG.

CAPTAIN, L-LET'S GET OUT OF HERE!
ESSENCE NO! WITH OUR NEW LITTLE BUDDY HERE... WE'RE TAKING THE SHIP!

...AND A FEW MINUTES LATER, WE DID EXACTLY THAT. JERRREECKO ASKED ME TO JOIN HIS CREW AFTERWARDS.
...AND I KNOW THE REST. I AM GETTING BACK TO MY SHOW.
THANKS FOR SAVING US!
MY PLEASURE.

SO YOU JOINED HIS CREW... AND THAT MADE YOU WHAT? A PRIVATE INVESTIGATOR? COP?
BOUNTY HUNTER... MOSTLY. WE TOOK WHAT WORK WE COULD FIND.

BUT IT WENT SOUTH... FAST. NO SOONER HAD WE CAPTURED THEIR SHIP AND WERE BACK ONBOARD THE VANGUARD, DID WE FIND OURSELVES SURROUNDED BY ANOTHER GROUP. I WAS HIDDEN IN A STORAGE AREA BECAUSE IT'S ILLEGAL TO INTERFERE WITH PRIMITIVES. BUT WHEN I CAME BACK OUT WE WERE ELSEWHERE, THE McMACAZORKIANS WERE GONE AND THEY ALL STARTED CALLING ME A STOWAWAY. NO-ONE REMEMBERED ANYTHING, NOT EVEN SHIPWRECK!
WEIRD. WHY DIDN'T THEY JUST DROP YOU BACK TO YOUR HOME-WORLD, THEN?

"THEY DIDN'T REMEMBER EVER HAVING BEEN THERE!"
"SHIP'S LOG?"
"...SHOWED THEY WERE IN HYPERSPACE THE WHOLE TIME. ALTHOUGH STRETCH - THE ENGINEER - SAID THAT DIDN'T MAKE MUCH SENSE, CONSIDERING THE DISTANCE... BUT IT MATCHED WHAT THEY REMEMBERED."

"SO NO-ONE KNOWS WHERE YOU CAME FROM? WHERE YOUR WORLD IS?"
"NO."

"I'M... SO SORRY. BUT HOW DID YOU GET OUT HERE, ON TARS STATION?"
"WELL, WE HAD A LOT OF ADVENTURES. AND BEING A STOW-AWAY MEANT THEY WEREN'T RESPONSIBLE FOR ME BEING OFF-WORLD. MAYBE THAT WAS THEIR EXCUSE, I DON'T KNOW. BUT I WAS TOO HANDY IN A FIGHT FOR THEM TO NOT KEEP ME AROUND."

"AT FIRST IT WAS FUN. FINALLY SOMETHING I WAS GOOD AT. WHAT HAD MADE ME AN OUTCAST BACK HOME NOW MADE ME A HERO. IT FELT GOOD CAPTURING CRIMINALS AND TURNING THEM IN. HECK, WE CAPTURED GOBBY TWICE!"
"GOBBY? THIS GOBBY? HOW ARE YOU STILL FRIENDS?"
"WE WERE JUST DOING OUR JOBS. AND WE ALL TREATED HIM WITH RESPECT (WELL EXCEPT FOR JERRREECKO - HE HATES CRYSTALLONIANS). I MEAN, CRIMINALS ARE STILL PEOPLE AND FRANKLY WE WEREN'T MUCH BETTER."

"SOME OF THE JOBS WE TOOK... I DON'T KNOW WHO WAS WORSE: THE "SCUM" WE CAUGHT OR THE SCUM WE SOLD THEM TO. I WAS... LOSING MY SENSE OF WHO I WAS."

"THEY KEPT PUSHING ME, ENCOURAGING THE WORST PARTS OF ME, UNTIL...."
GOOD JOB LITTLE BUDDY!

"WHEN A JOB BROUGHT US HERE TO TARS STATION... I... IT FELT LIKE... A PLACE I BELONGED. SO I STAYED."
I'M NOT LEAVING Y---
WHAM!
I'M STAYING!
OKAY! OKAY! ...SUIT YOURSELF!

YOU EXILED YOURSELF HERE? WITH THE WORST 'SCUM' IN THE GALAXY?
IT'S... WHERE I BELONG.
BRUTE... KODEE... YOU CAN'T LET YOUR MISTAKES DEFINE YOU.
OF COURSE I CAN! IT'S WHO I AM. NOTHING BUT AN ANGRY BRUTE!

WELL YOU'RE THE "BRUTE" THAT JUST SAVED MY LIFE!
SO DID GOBBY. HE'S STILL A WANTED KILLER.

LISTEN, I'VE MADE A BUNCH OF BAD DECISIONS. ONE FOOLISH ONE COST ME 4 YEARS OF MY LIFE - AS A SLAVE. BUT THOUGH MY BODY WAS A SLAVE, MY MIND NEVER WAS. BECAUSE I KNOW THAT I WAS CREATED TO BE MORE THAN THAT... MORE THAN THIS.

MAYBE YOU WENT FROM BEING 'THE BIGGEST, MOST ORNERY CUSS'ON YOUR PLANET TO THE TOUGHEST,MOST ORNERY CUSS IN THE WHOLE GALAXY BECAUSE YOU'VE BEEN CALLED TO DO SOMETHING GREATER WITH YOUR LIFE.

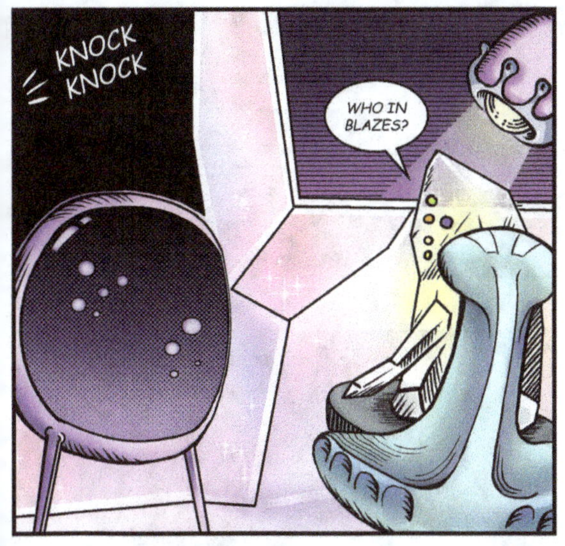

KNOCK KNOCK
WHO IN BLAZES?

WHAT DO YOU WANT?
HI SIR. SORRY TO BOTHER YOU. I'M A SIMPLE MERCHANT LOOKING TO FIND MY ESCAPED SLAVES. HAVE YOU SEEN THEM?

WHAT? NO. GET LOST!
THAT'S HIM, BOSS.
REALLY? 'CAUSE I DO BELIEVE YOU HAVE SEEN THEM.

I'M WARNING YOU: YOU HAVE 3 SECONDS TO GET OFF MY PROPERTY. 1... 2...
B-BUT I JUST WANT TO TALK...

...3!!
THIS IS A PORCUPINIAN SONIC BLASTER. AT MY COMMAND YOU CAN BE SHATTERED INTO A MILLION SHARDS. NOW... LET ME ASK AGAIN: HAVE YOU SEEN MY SLAVES?
KRRREEESSH

KNOCK KNOCK
UH... BRUTE? IT'S GOBBY HERE. YOUR RENT IS PAST DUE.
WHAT ARE YOU TALKING ABOUT? I PAID YOU AL--

--READY? WHO?
I'M SO SORRY DUDE.

OH CRA---- ARRRGGH!
CLINK!
GOT YA!

NOW YOU'RE GOING TO PAY FOR STEALING MY SLAVE! NOTHING CAN WITH--STAND A CRABI'S CLAW CRUSH!
JORJ NO!
TO BE CONTINUED.
JOIN US NEXT ISSUE FOR THE PULSE-POUNDING, ACTION-PACKED CONCLUSION!

eSq
COMICS

#3
THE TOUGHEST "TEDDY BEAR" IN THE GALAXY
BRUTE
BRUTE & THE GANG VS. JORJ & HIS GOONS!
YOU'RE ONE NANOSECOND AWAY FROM THE ASTEROID-SHAKING BATTLE YOU THOUGHT COULD WELL HAPPEN!
KEENAN NEWHART
(AFTER INFANTINO & ANDERSON)

TARS STATION. A PIRATE BASE ASTEROID OUTSIDE OF THE MILKY WAY.
NOTHING CAN WITHSTAND A CRABI'S CLAW CRUSH! *UGH* WHY ARE YOU SO *HUFF* HEAVY?
LET HIM GO JORJ - IT'S ME YOU WANT!
I'M SO SORRY...
SHUT UP AND ENJOY THE SHOW.
AAAAAAAGH!!
PRICE OF FREEDOM
OKAY FOLKS - THAT'S ME, GETTING A PAINFUL REMINDER AS TO WHY I SHOULDN'T STICK MY MUZZLE INTO OTHER PEOPLE'S BUSINESS. THE PINK LADY IS ROSE, A SLAVE I HELPED ESCAPE. THE CRABI IS HER FORMER OWNER AND THE 3 BIG PLACTORIS ARE HIS GOONS. WHICH LEAVES THE CRYSTALONIAN KNOWN AS 'GREEN ORANGE BLUE BEIGE YELLOW' OR 'GOBBY' FOR SHORT - MY LANDLORD - WHO APPARENTLY RATTED US OUT TO SAVE HIS OWN HIDE. CAN'T SAY I BLAME HIM. AS FOR ME, THEY CALL ME 'BRUTE'... AND YOU'RE ABOUT TO FIND OUT WHY...
WRITTEN AND CREATED BY PRESTON SQUIRE
ILLUSTRATED AND LETTERED BY OWEN KEENAN
COLOUR ARTIST - BROOKE NEWHART

I'LL DEAL WITH *UFF* YOU IN A SEC! BUT FIRST, *OOOMPH* THIS ONE MUST PAY FOR *AH* STEALING MY SLAVE!
HE'S NOT PART OF THIS! FIGHT ME YOU SIDEWALKING CRACKIS CROOK!

SUCH HOSTILITY! *NNGH* HAVEN'T I ALWAYS TREATED YOU *HUFF* WELL?
YOU ENSLAVED ME! YOU STOLE 4 YEARS OF MY LIFE!

"STOLE ?!" YOU WERE *UGH* WELL-FED AND CARED-FOR! SHOW SOME GRATITUDE! I SAVED YOU!
SO YOU COULD WORK ME DAY & NIGHT, LOOKING AFTER YOU AND THESE LAZY, SLOPPY PIGS!!
WHAT'S A "PIG"?

CRACKIS! HOW ARE YOU SO TOUGH? I CAN CRUSH BOULDERS INTO DUST BUT I CAN'T SNAP YOUR LITTLE LEG?
LET... ME...

CRRCCKK!
..GO!
ARRRGH! MY SHELL!!!
HAH! PAYBACK!!

OH ESSENCE! CRACKIS! MY SHELL, MY PRECIOUS SHELL!
TAKE THAT!!
YEEOUCH - THAT CRABI GOT MY LEG GOOD!
KLANG!
I NEED A MEDIC...

LINNI, GRAB ROSE. TUBBS, YOU GUARD THIS ONE. IF HE SO MUCH AS GLOWS, SHATTER HIM! I'LL TAKE CARE OF THIS LITTLE FURBALL...
OKAY!
YEAH, GREAT...
SHRANK

OOOH... COME ON, GET UP! AAARGH!! GOTTA.... HELP ROSE!
HEY PIPSQUEAK!

EAT DIRT!
...HUH?
BACK OFF!!
OH COME ON! I SAW THAT COMING A MILE AWAY!
BLAM!

...NOW IT'S MY AARRCCK!! MY LEG!

CRACKIS! CRACKIS. GET UP!!

GOTCHA!
BRUTE!
THUD!

HANDS OFF, LINNI!!
OWWW!
MOROCK, YOU'RE MINE!
REALLY ROSE? YOU DON'T STAND A...
...CHANCE?
NO. NO... DON'T YOU -- AAAAAAA !!
SWIPE!
SHUNK

GET OFF!
AARRRGH!
SNAP!
COME HERE, YOU...
OW! OW! OW!
I SAID... COME HERE!
HOP HOP HOP
WHAM!

ENOUGH
WITH THE
STABBY - STABBY!
CLANG!
LET...
ME...
GO!

NOW
HOLD STILL.
LINNI
COME COLLAR
HER!

NO!
NO!

SHE'S
SQUIRMING
TOO MUCH!
HELP!
HELP
ME!

RRROWR...
GIVE IT UP, ROSE!
THERE'S NO-ONE
TO SAVE YOU --
BRUTE!
GOBBY!
HELP ME!

---NOW?
HSST!
GRROOWR!
AAAAA!!
GET IT OFF!
GET IT OFF!

OOOOF
THUMP
I'VE GOT HIM, JORJ!
...JORJ?

ATTA BOY, CAESAR!
SNAP!
MROWR
GO---

RRRREEOWRR!!
---AWAY!

...I'LL TAKE IT FROM HERE...
OH PLEASE! GIVE IT UP, ALREADY!

GOT YA!
SNAP!
NOT THIS TIME!

GULP!*
PING
COLLAR HER, LINNI!

HOLD STILL...

OOPS.
CLICK
SERIOUSLY? YOU COLLARED MY PINCER?

JORJ! LOOK OUT!!
WHAT THE...?
GET OUT FROM THERE!

HA! RECOGNIZE THIS?
...SHE'S GOT THE COLLAR CONTROL...
TELL ME, JORJ... WILL THIS LIQUIFY YOUR CLAW LIKE IT WOULD'VE MY BRAIN?

ROSE... DON'T BE RASH. PUT IT DOWN. WE CAN... WE CAN WORK THIS OUT.
NOT A CHANCE.
CLIK

EEEECK !!
CLANK

YOU PATHETIC LITTLE FOOL! IT CAN'T PUNCTURE MY SHELL! NOW... NOW YOU'RE GOING TO...

WAHHHHGGGHH
--PAY...?
CRRRCK!
THUNK

ROSE! WATCH OUT!
LINNI- GET HER!
OOOFF!
BUMP!
COME HERE!
OOOH...
IT'S LEAKING...!!
I CAN'T FEEL MY CLAW!

I'VE GOT HER, JORJ!
TOLD YOU BEFORE: HANDS OFF THE LADY!
OOUUMPP!
THOOOM!
ROSE! YOU OKAY?
...I'LL LIVE...
YOU AGAIN? DIDN'T YOU LEARN?
COUGH COUGH

THIS TIME...

...STAY...
HOP

...DOW... NGH!
POW!

"DIDN'T I LEARN"? OH I LEARNED... HOW ABOUT YOU?
ACK! JORJ! JORJ! WHAT DO I DO?
GET US OUT OF HERE, LINNI!
...UNNGH...

QUICK! BACK TO THE SHIP!
OKAY JORJ!
HEY! WHERE'RE YOU GOING? WHAT ABOUT ME?

AH... YOU ALL STAY BACK, NOW! I'LL... I'LL KILL HIM!
WAIT... IS THAT A THREAT OR A BRIBE?
...HUH?...

LIKE EVERYONE HERE, GOBBY'S A WANTED CRIMINAL. YOU'D BE DOING THE FEDERATION A FAVOUR OFFING HIM.
...WHA?...
BUT I WON'T SPARE YOU 'CAUSE YOU DID IT - I'LL JUST HAVE TO HURT YOU MORE.

AHH... O-OKAY...
CLICK

AHH... LOOK, WHAT IF I JUST LET HIM GO? SEE, NO-ONE HAS TO GET HURT. WE GOOD?
I GUESS I'M OKAY WITH THAT. BUT IF YOU LET HIM GO, HE'S DEFINITELY GOING TO BLAST YOU.
WHAT?

YEAH. THAT'S TOUGH. I'D SUGGEST YOU SHOCK HIM... AND THEN RUN FOR YOUR LIFE.
YOU WON'T GET FAR, SO JUST TAKE YOUR BEATING LIKE A McMAC.

HUH?
FSSSSSST

...OH...

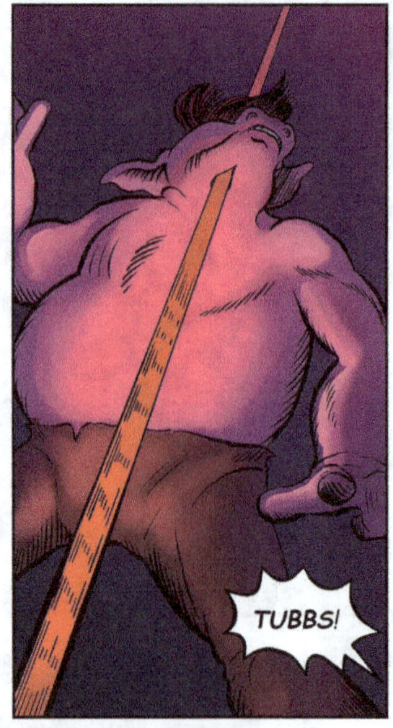

TUBBS!

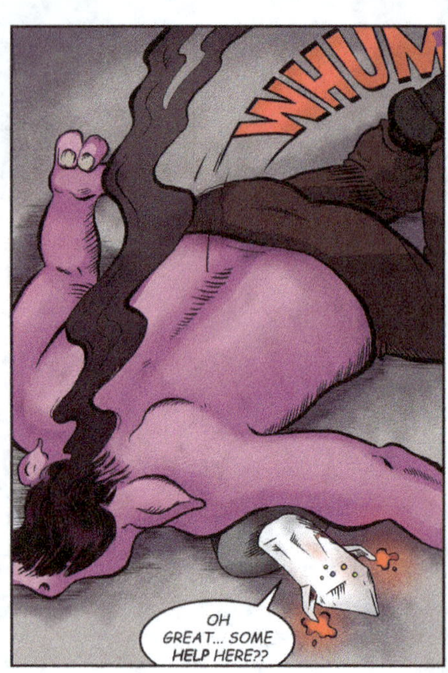

WHUM
OH GREAT... SOME HELP HERE??

WHAT THE CRACKIS, GOBBY?
OH TUBBS! ...I'M SORRY...
BUT GOBBY--- HOW DID YOU...? I SAW YOUR ARMS SHATTERED!
I RE-GREW THEM WHILE BRUTE KEPT HIM DISTRACTED, MELTED THE BLASTER AND THEN...

YOU DIDN'T HAVE TO KILL HIM!
OH PLEASE... NOBODY DOES THAT TO ME AND GETS AWAY WITH IT!

FREE! ...AH CRACKIS...
WHAT?
POOR TUBBS!

COME HERE.
ROSE!

GET BACK OR I'LL SNAP HER NECK!
MOROCK... DON'T. PLEASE LET ME GO.
DON'T WORRY ROSE. I'VE GOT YOU.
I CAN GET HIM IN ONE SHOT, ROSE!
LET HER GO OR I'LL...

NO! GOBBY, DON'T!

STAY BACK, YOU!

MOROCK STOP! DON'T DO THIS!

I'M TAKING YOU HOME, ROSE. JORJ WILL BE VERY HAPPY WITH ME.
NO! I CAN'T GO BACK. I CAN'T! PLEASE!

IT'S OKAY. JORJ WILL TAKE CARE OF YOU.
OH MOROCK...
...I'M SO SORRY...
HEY MOROCK - JORJ SAYS YOU'RE A BIG MOUTH!
ACK!
HE WHA--
BOOMF!
NNNNHH....
WHOA!
ROSE!
RELAX...
...GOT YOU!
THANKS!

YOU... KILLED HIM?
NO. IT'S JUST KNOCK-OUT GAS. HE'LL BE FINE.
OH YEAH?

FFFZZZZTT!

GOBBY!! CRACKIS! HE WAS OUT! YOU HAD NO REASON TO--
DON'T LECTURE ME, BOUNTY HUNTER. HOW MANY LIVES HAVE YOU TAKEN, JUST TO MAKE A CRED?

UH... YEAH... WELL...
...THOUGHT SO.

AH... YOUR HUMAN HAS SPRUNG A LEAK.
ROSE? YOU OKAY? WHAT'S WRONG?
THEY'RE... DEAD. AND IT'S MY FAULT.

OH, THAT'S TOTALLY GOBBY'S FAULT.
THEY WOULDN'T BE DEAD IF I HADN'T RUN AWAY.

SO WHAT? THEY ENSLAVED YOU! THEY DESERVED IT!
GOBBY!

LOOK, WE CRYSTALONIANS HAVE A SAYING: "THE LIGHT OF THOSE YOU'VE LOST IS NOW YOURS TO CARRY."
HUH?
IT MEANS SHE NEEDS TO SHINE EVEN BRIGHTER, SO THE WORLD IS LESS DARK WITHOUT THEM.

SHE'S NOT A CRYSTALONIAN! SHE CAN'T "SHINE"!
NO BRUTE... I... THINK HE MEANS I NEED TO DO SOMETHING WORTHWHILE WITH MY LIFE... SO THE LOSS OF THEIRS' WASN'T IN VAIN.
CLEVER, CARBON!

OH.
BUT WHAT CAN I DO? I'M NOTHING SPECIAL.

... I COULD GET YOU A JOB... MAYBE.
A JOB?
YEAH, AT THE BAR I WORK AT. WOULD YOU LIKE THAT?
... YES. PLEASE.

BY THE ESSENCE! IF YOU'RE GOING TO SPEND THE REST OF YOUR EXISTENCE ON THIS ROCK, SERVING CHEAP BEER TO EVEN CHEAPER PIRATES, YOU'D HAVE BEEN BETTER OFF STAYING A SLAVE.
ROSE...

...YOU SAID... THAT I WAS MEANT FOR SOME-THING GREATER. I DON'T KNOW ABOUT THAT. BUT I THINK THAT YOU ARE. MAYBE GOBBY AND I DESERVE TO BE HERE... BUT YOU DON'T. YOU'RE BETTER THAN ALL OF THIS.

THANKS... FOR EVERY-THING.

NO. THANK ME WHEN I GET YOU OFF THIS ROCK!
WHAT? HOW?
I DON'T KNOW. BUT THIS IS NO PLACE FOR YOU... I'M GOING TO GET YOU HOME!

EPILOGUE 1: MEANWHILE, BACK IN THE MILKY WAY GALAXY, DOMOKA, NEW PUMIKA CITY, WE FIND A RAG-TAG BAND OF WOULD-BE BOUNTY HUNTERS.
THEY'RE BACK.
STATUS REPORT?
AS USUAL, YOU'VE PUT US IN AN IMPOSSIBLE SITUATION.
THE PLACE IS MORE HEAVILY GUARDED THAN A CRABI BANK! WE ARE NOT GETTING IN THERE!

THE CAPTAIN'S GOT A PLAN; HE'S ALWAYS GOT A PLAN.
...JUST NEVER A SANE ONE.
SHUT UP, SHIPWRECK! WE'LL FIND A WAY. OR WE'LL MAKE ONE.

WE'D NEED A HUNDRED MEN... BUT BEFORE WE GO BUSTING IN, ARE WE EVEN SURE HE'S STILL IN THERE?
SHIPWRECK?
WE HAD MULTIPLE SIGHTINGS OF HIM ENTERING THE BUNKER A WEEK AGO. NO SIGNS OF HIM SINCE. ERGO - HE'S STILL THERE.
...UNLESS HE'S GOT SOME GETTAWAY TUNNEL OR TRANSPORTER OR SUCH AND HE'S LONG GONE.
IT'S TOO BAD WE DON'T HAVE A DOPPLEGÄNGER OR WRAITH WITH US TO SNEAK IN AND SEE IF HE'S STILL THERE.

THAT'S BRILLIANT, STRETCH!
THANKS VAN -- CAPTAIN!... SIR! IT WOULD BE IF WE HAD ANYONE ABLE TO AH...
...WHY IS EVERYONE LOOKING AT ME?

OH... NO. NOOOO. ESSENCE NO. NOT HAPPENING. NO CRACKIS WAY!
YOU'RE TOTALLY GOING.
OH, COME ON!

EPILOGUE 2: ON THE PLANTIS HOME-WORLD 'EDEN', IN THE HIGH PALACE OF THE CHURCH OF THE EVERLASTING ESSENCE.
GRAND CHANCELLOR, YOU SUMMONED?
RINTAX, IT'S GOOD TO SEE YOU, OLD APPRENTICE! BUT IT WAS NOT I WHO SUMMONED YOU; IT WAS THE COUNCIL OF ELDERS.
THE COUNCIL? SUMMONED ME?
YOU ARE AN ADEPT; ONE OF OUR BEST. DON'T BE SO SHOCKED. YOU ARE WORTHY. GO ON... THEY'RE WAITING.

ENTER, RINTAX.
HOW MAY I SERVE?
YOU ARE FAMILIAR WITH THIS WORLD?
YES. MY LAST DISCIPLE WAS FROM THERE.

THEN YOU KNOW OF THEIR PREDICAMENT?
YES. THEY ARE ON THE VERGE OF LOSING ALL CONNECTION TO THE ESSENCE.
THEY HAVE REQUESTED HELP.
BUT... GALACTIC LAW PROHIBITS INTER-FERING. SURELY THIS COUNCIL...

THIS COUNCIL WILL DO NOTHING. YOU WILL.
I...? WILL WHAT?
YOU WILL LEAD AN ELITE, COVERT FORCE TO SAVE THEM.
I AM SWORN TO PEACE! YOU CAN'T...

YOU QUESTION THE ESSENCE?
THE... ESSENCE... SAID THAT?
YES. WE ALL FELT IT; YOU WERE CHOSEN FOR THIS TASK. ARE YOU NOT SWORN TO OBEY THE ESSENCE?
YES... OF COURSE.
THEN GO. YOU ARE RELEASED FROM ALL YOUR DUTIES HERE.
REPORT BACK PERIODICALLY.

SOOO... HOW DID IT GO?
I... I... ESSENCE GIVE ME COURAGE, FOR I AM PETRIFIED!

Brute

Real Name: Kodee a Kamis
Race: Unknown - unofficially classified as 'Bruin' by Rose Kahn
Height: 2' tall
Weight: 1440 lbs
Birthplace: Undocumented world he calls 'Bru'
History: According to Captain Jerreeecko Brute was a stowaway aboard his vessel, however, Brute tells a very different tale of having saved Jerreecko's life and having been invited to join the crew - a story no one can corroborate.
Profession: Bouncer, pugilist, claims to have been an ice miner on Bru.
Temperament: Good natured, sweet, bold, straight talking, cocky, easily offended and quick to anger.
Abilities: Brute's homeworld is unknown but based on his physical make-up it's gravity is far stronger than life should be able to exist on. Due to the crushing gravity of his homeworld Brute is the strongest being in the galaxy, has incredibly quick reflexes, is extremely dense, nearly impenetrable, and a particularly small stature for his mass (which makes him look far more harmless than he is).

Due to the cold climate of his native Bru, water only exists in liquid form along the equator. Therefore bruins have evolved with the ability to generate signigant heat from their palms (and feet), enough to melt ice that'd otherwise be trapped as permafrost. With concentrated effort, by cupping his hands Brute can create a plasma ball of super-charged air.

Like all bruins, Brute is comfortable in temperatures well below freezing, insulated by thick fur and padded feet.

Equipment: Brute wears a belt that is a high tech multi-purpose device similar to a holographic cellphone. It also controls his personal gravity field allowing him to exist in his native gravity, or lowering it so he can make huge leaps.

Rose

Real Name: Rosita Maria Kahn
Race: Human from Earth
Height: 5' 11' tall
Weight: 160 lbs
Birthplace: Queezzeenee Research Space Station

History: Rose is the first-born to human scientists, (Maria Santiago & Muthan Kahn), who were living aboard a remote intergalactic research station studying an anomaly. Eldest of 5 children, her family were the only humans Rose has even known. Once she turned 14, her parents decided to send her to Earth for a year to learn human culture. After leaving for Earth the research station was attacked and destroyed and Rose ended up being abandoned on an intergalactic space station. She had to learn to survive on her own, with only her cat, Caesar, to depend on (somewhat... cat's are fickle).

Profession: Bartender, slave, bounty hunter

Temperament: Sweet, kind-hearted, and compassionate but hardened by many betrayals of trust. Bold, untrusting, and overly self-reliant. Unafraid to go after what she wants.

Abilities: Rose is taught in intergalactic martial arts, swordsmanship

Equipment: Rose wields two swords and carries a range of rose-shaped grenades each with it's own unique properties. Her color-coded grenades include: Concussive, smokescreen, flash, electric, and knockout gas.

Companion: Rose is often accompanied by her feline companion, Caesar. A male, british-blue cat who (when traveling) stays within eyesight of his human, and isn't afraid to jump into a fray if she seems to be in trouble.

Jorj & Linni

Real Name: Jorj (and Linni)
Race: Crabi / Plactori
Height: 3' (Jorj), 20' (Linni)
Weight: 280 lbs (Jojh), 13 tons (Linni)
Birthplace: Unknown
History: Little is known about Jorj's early life. He was a intergalactic trader for some time, specializing in trade on fringe worlds and outposts like Earth, Moohoovan Station and Tars Station. He employs three plactori crewmen; the dimwitted (even by plactori standards) Linni, the war vet Morock, and the slovenly Tubbs. He's also known to abduct homeless beings to use as slave labor.
Profession: Captain of the Abundance (spaceship), trader of illicit goods.
Temperament: Jorj is personable and a smooth talker. He genuinely cares for those in his care, crew and slave alike and strives to be a good boss/owner. Like all crabi Jorj is primarily money-driven and always looking to make more money (and spend as little as possible). He is duplicitous and even the truth is distorted to serve his purposes. He's a great guy to have a drink with, but do not buy any 'prime' real estate from him...
Abilities: Con man with a pleasing personality and smooth talker. Like all crabi he's has a protective shell that can withstand tremendous physical trauma and a large pincer claw that can crush rocks or easily tear a plactori's foot clean off. Even McMacazorkians (the strongest known race in the galaxy) fear a crabi's claw crush. Crabi's can live equally well in air or water environments.
Equipment: None of note.
Companion: Jorj's longest and most loyal companion is **Linni**, his plactori indentured servant, who has been with him since he was a young crabi. While Jorj often employs other plactori indentured servants (recently Morock and 'Tubbs'), Linni holds a special place in Jorj's heart, despite, or perhaps due to, his ineptitude.

Vanguard

Real Name: Captain Jerrreecko Krrrsskyk

Race: Porcupinian

Height: 7'6" tall (9' to tip of quills)

Weight: 375 lbs

Birthplace: Grrrithkathk-Ckirrrggik (roughly translates into 'Battle of Blood River City')

History: Vanguard speaks very little about his past. What is known is he was dishonorably discharged from the porcupinian military (where all young porcupinians serve a term). As honor is incredibly important to porcupinians, Vanguard seeks to redeem his by becoming a bounty hunter of distinction. So far, despite his silver quills (a mark of distinction), porcupinian warship and (somewhat delusional) self-confidence allowing him to hire a crew of compentent bouty hunters, he has yet to produce note-worthy results as a bounty hunter.

Profession: Captain of the Vanguard (spaceship), bounty hunter, mercenary. Formerly porcupinian military.

Temperament: He's a jerk. He knows he's a jerk. If you have a problem with it, that's your problem. Takes care of his crew, like family. Tactical genius but very impulsive and seldom thinks the consequences of his actions through.

Abilities: Like all porcupinians, Vanguard is stronger than a human (about equal to a gorilla), double-jointed, covered in quills, and has superior senses of sight, smell and hearing. He's also military trained, sharp-shooter and surf-boarder.

Equipment: Vanguard typically wields two duo barreled blasters, along with a waist mounted ion cannon.

Companion: A 'compupal' unit he's termed '**Shipwreck**' which is a non-senient AI unit capable of providing intel on a huge number of topics, performing various feats, and flying via anti-gravity units on it's base. It can also carry a load, including Vanguard himself, while flying.

COMICS
ISSUE #0
THE TOUGHEST "TEDDY BEAR" IN THE GALAXY
BRUTE
YOU WANT HER? YOU'LL HAVE TO GO THROUGH ME!

"SUPPLY RUN"

WRITTEN BY: PRESTON SQUIRE
ILLUSTRATED BY: OWEN KEENAN

AFTER MONTHS OF TRAVELING, THE SPACESHIP **VANGUARD** HAS FINALLY REACHED **MOOHOOVAN STATION** IN THE PEGASUS ARM OF THE GALAXY EN ROUTE TO EARTH. AMONG THOSE ON BOARD ARE **ROSE KHAN** - HUMAN - MELEE AND EXPLOSIVES EXPERT AND HER BEST FRIEND KODEE A.K.A. **BRUTE** - BRUIN - PUGILIST FROM A HIGH GRAVITY WORLD...

SO YOU USED TO LIVE HERE?
YEARS AGO. THE SHIP THAT WAS SUPPOSED TO TAKE ME TO EARTH DITCHED ME HERE
WERE THERE OTHER HUMANS?
THIS IS THE OUTERMOST RANGE OF HUMAN SPACE TRAVEL, SO THEY DID CARRY HUMAN SUPPLIES. BUT I NEVER SAW ONE MYSELF.
IT'S OUR STOP.
WHOAH!
OH MY GOSH!
THE HUMAN SUPPLIES VENDOR WAS JUST AROUND THIS CORNER...

"THERE'S MEN, HUMAN MEN!"
"THAT'S A HUMAN MALE? DIDN'T THINK THEY'D BE SO HANDSOMELY HAIRY!"
"THAT'S A GORILLA."

OH... WELL LET'S GO TALK TO THEM!
I'VE... NEVER TALKED TO A MAN BEFORE... OTHER THAN MY DAD...
REALLY? WOW...

LET'S GET YOU MATED!
WAIT... WHAT?!
DON'T BE SHY. ALL RACES MATE. WELL... ALMOST ALL.

NO, IT'S NOT THAT. IT'S JUST... THAT... WELL... I KIND OF THOUGHT... MAYBE...

LET'S GO!

HI !
WHO ARE YOU?
WHAT YOU WANT? SUPPLIES OURS NOW.
WHERE DID YOU COME FROM?
I'M ROSE. I'M FROM THE VANGUARD. WE'RE ON OUR WAY TO EARTH.
AREN'T YOU A CUTE LITTLE FELLA!
WHAT?
TO EARTH? NOT FROM EARTH?
I WAS BORN ON A RESEARCH STATION.
WAIT! YOU'RE TRAVELING WITH ALIENS? NO. YOU'RE COMING WITH US.
NO ROO...
BRUTE?!

NO, TO EARTH. MY FIRST TIME, ACTUALLY!
IT TALKS! WHAT'S YOUR NAME?
BRUTE.
HA HA HA HA HA HA

KEEP LAUGHING AND I'LL SHOW YOU WHY I'M CALLED THAT!

YOU'RE COMING WITH US!
UNHAND ME!
SIGH YOU ASKED FOR IT...
AW, LOOK, HER PET'S MAD. CUTE.

SMAK!
SHE SAID LET GO!

SMAK!
NO HURT HUMANS!

HEY! LETGO!
UMPH! TEDDY HEAVY!
BRUTE, WATCH OUT!

KLANG!!

OKAY THEN...

...NO WAY...
THUD!
CRASH!
WHAM!

SMASH!
WHOAH! RUN!

ANYONE ELSE THINK I'M CUTE?

IDIOTS HAD IT COMING. BUT... I WAS HOPING TO GET YOU MATED UP.
HA! TRUE. AND WE GOT EACH OTHER.
STOP THAT. AT LEAST THEY LEFT ME ALL THESE SUPPLIES.

BRUTE
PART TWO: "BUYER'S REMORS[E]"
WRITTEN AND CREATED BY: PRESTON SQUIRE.
ILLUSTRATED BY: OWEN KEENAN
EN ROUTE TO EARTH, THE STARSHIP VANGUARD HAS DOCKED AT MOOHOOVAN STATION. CAPTAIN JERRREECKO LET HUMAN ROSE KHAN AND BRUIN KODEE (AKA 'BRUTE') GO FETCH SOME HUMAN SUPPLIES.
A DECISION HE'S REGRETTING...
I TOLD YOU TO GET SOME SUPPLIES - NOT BUY OUT THE STORE.
I LEFT SOME.
HARDLY.
BRUTE COPYRIGHT 2020 eSq COMICS.   WWW.BRUTECOMIC.COM

WHAT THE CRAKIS ARE THESE?
WHY DO YOU NEED A WHOLE CARTON OF PADS?
THEY'RE PADS.
I USE THEM MONTHLY.

OOOHHH!! OH, YEAH. YEAH. YOU NEED THESE.
BUT YOU DON'T NEED A CARTON...

I HAVEN'T BEEN ABLE TO GET HUMAN SUPPLIES IN YEARS. I THOUGHT--
WE'RE HEADED TO DIRT Y'KNOW.
IT'S CALLED EARTH.
THAT'S WHAT I SAID.

ANYWAY, THERE'S NO STORAGE SPACE FOR THIS, IT'LL ALL HAVE TO GO IN YOUR ROOM.
ON TOP. I DON'T CARE. FIGURE IT OUT.
MY CLOSET OF A ROOM? WHERE AM I SUPPOSED TO SLEEP?

THAT'S NOT FAIR.
FAIR? WHAT'S NOT FAIR IS YOUR TAKING A ROOM THAT I COULD'VE GIVEN TO A REAL WARRIOR.

YOUR DIRT EXPERTISE BETTER BE WORTH IT.
IT'S...

...EARTH.

YOU OKAY?
YEAH... WELL... NO.

YOU CONVINCED HIM I'M AN EXPERT ON EARTH. I'M NOT. HIS COMPUPAL PROBABLY KNOWS MORE THAN I DO.
SO?

SO? WHEN HE REALIZES I'M NOT, HE'LL KICK ME OFF THE SHIP!
HE WON'T REALIZE UNTIL WE'RE ON EARTH. AND THEN, SO WHAT? ...

... YOU'RE HOME.

BUT... I WANT TO STAY. I WANT TO HELP. IT'S MY HOMEWORLD. I SHOULD HELP.
THEN HELP. I KNOW YOU'RE A BETTER FIGHTER THAN HE'S GIVING YOU CREDIT FOR.

I HAVE TO GO BACK.
GO BACK?

I HAVE TO TALK TO THOSE GUYS. THEY KNOW EARTH FIRST-HAND.
THOSE... YOU MEAN THE HUMANS I BEAT UP?

YES, THOSE GUYS YOU BEAT UP.

I DON'T THINK...
I KNOW!

I'M GOING BACK. PLEASE BE A PAL AND PUT THIS STUFF IN MY ROOM FOR ME.
YOU'RE NOT GOING ALONE.

I'M COMING WITH--
THEY WON'T TALK TO YOU. AND I'M NOT GOING ALONE. CAESAR WILL BE WITH ME.
MEOW.

ROSE...
DON'T FOLLOW ME.

WELCOME BACK ROSE! I HOPE YOU DIDN'T FORGET ANYTHING, 'CAUSE I'VE NOTHING LEFT.
THOSE HUMANS BOUGHT UP THE REST?
YEAH. OH THEY WERE FURIOUS YOU BOUGHT UP ALL THE FOOD.
DO YOU KNOW WHERE THEY WENT?
THAT WAY. DON'T KNOW WHAT DOCK, BUT THEY BILLED IT TO THE... UM... SMS SAMUEL HEARNE.
SAMUEL HEARNE?
YOU KNOW IT?
...NO. BUT IT SEEMS ...FAMILIAR.
ANYWAY, I SHOULD BE ABLE TO LOCATE IT. THANKS!
ANYTIME ROSE!

HEY OFFICER LULLUMON.

ROSE! I HAVEN'T SEEN YOU IN A QUARIN'S AGE!
I HEARD YOU'D FINALLY FOUND A RIDE TO EARTH!
YEAH, THAT, AH, DIDN'T PAN OUT.

OH... I'M SORRY. WHAT BRINGS YOU BACK TO MOOHOOVAN STATION?
WITH A NEW CREW. REALLY AM EN ROUTE TO EARTH NOW. BUT FIRST... I NEED TO FIND THE SMS SAMUEL HEARNE.

WELL THAT'S EASY...
SMS SAMUEL HEARNE

BRUTE
EN ROUTE TO EARTH, THE STARSHIP VANGUARD HAS DOCKED AT MOOHOOVAN STATION. CAPTAIN JERRREECKO LET HUMAN ROSE KHAN AND BRUIN KODEE (AKA 'BRUTE') GO FETCH SOME HUMAN SUPPLIES. THEY ENDED UP GETTING INTO A VIOLENT CONFRONTATION WITH THE CREW OF THE EARTH SHIP SMS SAMUEL HEARNE.
ONLY AFTERWARDS DID ROSE REALIZE SHE'D NEED THEIR FIRST-HAND EARTH KNOWLEDGE; KNOWLEDGE SHE'S NOW SWORN TO GET.
COME ON CAESAR. OFFICER LULLUMON SAID THE SAMUEL HEARNE IS RIGHT OVER HERE.
THAT'S HER, SIR! AND SHE'S ALONE....
ME-OW.
LIVING LEGEND
PART THREE "LIVING LEGEND" BY PRESTON SQUIRE & OWEN KEENAN.
BRUTE COPYRIGHT 2020 ESQ COMICS WWW.BRUTECOMIC.COM

GRAB HER!
SMACK!
URK!
OOOH!
THUD!

AAHH!
GIRL TOUGH...

...BUT SOCRATES TOUGHER!
HSSSST!
LET ME GO! YOU DAMN DIRTY APE!

BAD KITTY! BAD KITTY!

WULP!
ALLEY-OOP!

HERE, CATCH.
THAT'LL BE QUITE ENOUGH.
ENOUGH? YOU ATTACKED ME! I CAME TO TALK.

TO TALK? RETURN THOSE SUPPLIES YOU STOLE FROM US!
I BOUGHT THOSE SUPPLIES.
MA'AM, YOU'RE IN NO POSITION TO ARGUE. YOU'RE OUTNUMBERED FOUR TO ONE.
IT'S A ROSE.

BOOMF!

YOU WERE SAYING?
...WHAT DID YOU WANT TO TALK ABOUT?

MY CREW ARE DEPENDING ON MY EXPERTISE ON EARTH, BUT... I'VE NEVER BEEN THERE BEFORE. I... I NEED YOUR FIRST-HAND KNOWLEDGE.

YOU'VE NEVER...? HOW IS THAT POSSIBLE?
MY PARENTS WERE SCIENTISTS. I WAS BORN ON A RESEARCH STATION. FAR FROM HERE. FAR FROM EARTH.
THEN IT'S AS WE FEARED...

WHY ARE YOU HOLDING MY CREW-MEMBER AT GUNPOINT?

CAPTAIN. I'M CAPTAIN FEI-TAN QUON. YOUR MAN THERE ASSAULTED MY CREW AND THEN THEY TOOK OUR SUPPLIES.
FEI-TAN...?

MY MAN? YOU MEAN THIS TINY, LITTLE GUY ...BEAT UP YOUR ENTIRE CREW?
YES.
WOW.

HE'S SUPER-STRONG.
OH, I KNOW. IT'S JUST US PORCUPINIANS WOULD NEVER ADMIT TO THAT.

SO YOU'VE NEVER LOST A FIGHT TO HIM?
WHAT? NO.
ACTUALLY...
SHUT-UP, $#!^HEAD.

FEI-TAN...
WE NEED THOSE SUPPLIES. I'M ASKING YOU TO RETURN THEM.
* YAWN * YOU LEFT THEM. SHE BOUGHT THEM. FAIR.

OH MY GOD! CAPTAIN FEI-TAN OF THE SAMUEL HEARNE!!
DON'T MAKE ME HURT THIS GIRL...

YES! WELL, I KNOW OF HIM. I STUDIED HIM IN HISTORY CLASS.
YOU KNOW HIM?

SO... EARTH DEVELOPED FASTER SPACE TRAVEL SINCE WE LEFT THEN? WE'RE NOT THE FIRST HUMANS HERE?

I GOT HERE 8 YEARS AGO, AND I WASN'T FIRST BY A LONG SHOT.
SINCE YOU LEFT, EARTH DISCOVERED FASTER WARP SPEEDS: 100 YEARS AGO AND AGAIN, BEFORE THE GREAT WAR.

GREAT WAR? WHAT HAPPENED? PLEASE, TELL US WHAT'S BEEN HAPPENING ON EARTH. ITS BEEN 200 YEARS SINCE WE LEFT!

I... YOU WANT ME TO...
AH, CRAKIS.

SORRY TO INTERRUPT, BUT I NEED MY CREW BACK. UNLIKE YOU, I DON'T HAVE 200 YEARS TO GET TO EARTH.

THE SUPPLIES. OR ELSE.
HARM HER, AND YOU'LL ANSWER TO ME.
WANT ME TO FINISH THIS?

NO BRUTE. I WILL.
I'LL GIVE YOU THE FOOD SUPPLIES.
THANK YOU.

WHAT THE CRAKIS! I JUST CARRIED IT ALL TO THE SHIP AND THESE JOKERS TRIED TO ABDUCT YOU!
BRUTE, RELAX. IT'S FINE.

BRUTE'S GOT A POINT. THAT'S WHY WE CAME.
I APOLOGIZE FOR MY MEN'S BEHAVIOR. THEY HAD NO RIGHT TO GRAB YOU.
I KNOW. IT'S JUST... HUMANS FROM THIS TIME PERIOD WERE PRETTY XENOPHOBIC.

SO... THEY'RE JERKS, BUT IT'S OKAY... 'CAUSE THEY'RE OLD JERKS?
BRUTE. I'M NOT CONDONING THEIR BEHAVIOUR. NOR AM I CONDONING MY OWN.

YOU DIDN'T DO ANYTHING! I'M THE ONE THAT KICKED THEIR BUTTS!
I SHOULDN'T HAVE BOUGHT ALL THE FOOD. NOR SHOULD I HAVE MADE YOU CARRY IT ALL. I WAS BEING SELFISH.

I DIDN'T MIND! YOU WERE SO HAPPY TO HAVE HUMAN FOOD!
I AM! AND I WILL KEEP SOME. BUT I'M USED TO ALIEN FOOD. I ENJOY IT. EVEN JERRREECKO'S COOKING!
WELL THAT'S A FIRST!

CAPTAIN FEI-TAN, YOU'RE A LEGEND. AND I'M SORRY YOUR MISSION DIDN'T TURN OUT AS YOU'D HOPED, BUT I SO ADMIRE YOU AND YOUR CREW FOR COMMITTING YOUR LIVES TO IT. SELLING YOU BACK THE FOOD IS THE LEAST I CAN DO.
THANK YOU ROSE. YOU GIVE ME HOPE FOR THE FUTURE OF HUMANITY.
...BUT, TELL ME... WHY ARE YOU PINK?
THE END

UM
THE
LAST

"AS FAR AS YOU KNOW, YOU ARE
THE LAST OF YOUR KIND...
LOM

...A PEOPLE LOST TO TIME. DISPLACED BY A DIFFERENT KIND OF PEOPLE WHO MAKE WORDS AND TOOLS. TO THEM, YOUR KIND ARE ALREADY JUST TALES OF BRUTES TOLD TO AMUSE OR FRIGHTEN CHILDREN... BUT TO THE YOUTH SAVING YOU NOW, YOU ARE AN ALL-TOO-REAL EGG THIEF!

GREEUNK!
THUNK!
THWIP!

KAW!
GRAWK!
THWIP!
THWIP!

GRAWWK!
GREEUNK!
YOU THERE!
DON'T MOVE OR I'LL STICK YOU LIKE I DID THAT GRYLAR!

AND WHAT MANNER OF MAN ARE YOU? THESE ARE AKARI LANDS. NEVER HAVE I SEEN YOUR LIKE.

LOM FACES HIS SAVIOUR. THE YOUTH HOLDS HIS WEAPON THREATENINGLY AND MAKES NOISES LOM DOESN'T UNDERSTAND, BUT HIS QUESTION IS CLEAR. LOM'S PEOPLE, NOW LOM ALONE, SPEAK NOT IN WORDS, BUT IN PURE THOUGHT.
THE GRYLAR EGGS BELONG TO WE AKARI. GO BACK TO YOUR TRIBE AND TELL THEM TO STAY AWAY!
I AM LOM. I WILL GO. LOM ALONE.
UNDER THE RAINBOW HUES OF THE SETTING SUN, THE YOUNG HUNTER, 'HAMI', FINDS HIS TALE OF FACING DOWN A MAGICAL 'TROLL' EGG-THIEF DOES NOT BRING HIM PRAISE FROM HIS ELDERS, BUT RIDICULE ...
HA HA
HA HA
HA HA
I TELL YOU IT'S TRUE! I SAW THE EGG-THIEF. IT'S A TROLL! HE PUTS WORDS IN ONE'S MIND, OKAY ???
HA
I BELIEVE YOU HAMI.
... THANK GOODNESS, THEN, FOR LITTLE SISTERS.
NEELA, 12, ADMIRES HER OLDER BROTHER, 15, LIKE NO OTHER. HAMI IS GRATEFUL THAT SOME-ONE BELIEVES IN HIM.
HA HA
NEELA, TOMORROW MORNING COME WITH ME TO THE CLIFFS. YOU AND I WILL CAPTURE THIS TROLL WHO CALLS HIMSELF 'LOM'!
REALLY? I'LL BE THERE!
THE AKARI, ONCE NOMADIC, HAVE BECOME FARMERS GROWING FRUITS AND VEGETABLES -- AND EVEN STARTING TO DOMESTICATE THE FIERCE GRYLARS FOR THEIR EGGS AND MEAT.
EARLY IN THE MORNING, HAMI AND NEELA SNEAK AWAY TO THE GRYLAR CLIFFS IN HOPES OF ONCE AGAIN SEEING THEIR MYSTERIOUS VISITOR.
THEY LOOK PRETTY RELAXED.
HMMM... THE GRYLARS DON'T SEEM WORRIED. I DON'T THINK THE TROLL HAS BEEN HERE YET...

WHICH SHELF DID YOU SEE THE TROLL ON HAMI?
WHY, THE TOP ONE OF COURSE! BUT DON'T WORRY, I'LL MAKE IT FUN.
COME ON, NEELA — I'LL RACE YOU TO THE TOP!
WHAT? HAMI! NO!
LAST ONE UP IS A ROTTEN EGG!
HAMI! WAIT UP!
NEVER ONE TO BACK DOWN FROM A CHALLENGE, NEELA RACES TO THE NEXT LADDER. THEY RAPIDLY CLIMB THE LADDERS WITH PRACTICED EASE...
COME ON, SLOWPOKE!
CHEATER! WAIT UP! NO FAIR!
CREAK!
...BUT A LONG, DRY SPELL HAS MADE THE LADDERS BRITTLE. NEELA IN HER HASTE STOMPS TOO HARD.
CRACK!
HAMI! I'M SLIPPING!
KAJA. GO UNDER GIRL.

NEELA GLANCES DOWN AND BEHOLDS AN UNBELIEVABLE SIGHT: A STRANGE HULKING CHARACTER — SURELY THIS MUST BE THE 'TROLL' OF WHICH HAMI SPOKE — SITTING ASTRIDE A MOUNTAIN OF A BEAST, UNLIKE ANYTHING EVEN THE TRIBE ELDERS DESCRIBED.
TERROR GRIPS HER AS THEY APPROACH, AND THEN... PEACE, AS SHE HEARS / FEELS KNOWS THIS 'TROLL' — LOM — IN HER MIND. THIS 'VOICE' SEEMS STRANGELY FAMILIAR... BUT SHE CAN'T POSSIBLY KNOW HIM.
HE'S YOUNG — HAMI'S AGE — AND EAGER TO MAKE AMENDS.
NOT A THIEF, JUST HUNGRY AND HAS SOMETHING TO RETURN.
NEELA TRUSTS THE 'VOICE', FEELS ITS SINCERITY... BUT HOW?
HE WILL SAVE HER... BUT WHY?
... AND WHO IS 'KAJA'?
I WON'T LET YOU FALL. LET GO NOW. KAJA CATCH.
HAMI! HELP ME!
AAAIEEEE!
NAB!
HELP — ... OH!
NEELA SAFE.
UM... HI THERE...

HAMI LOOKS ON, POWERLESS TO HELP AS HIS LITTLE SISTER FALLS AND IS CAUGHT BY THIS MYSTERIOUS 'TROLL'.

WHERE HAD HE COME FROM? WHAT IS THAT SHAGGY BEAST HE RIDES? FOR HIM TO BE THERE MEANT HE HAD TO BE VERY CLOSE WHEN THEY ARRIVED.

...HOW COULD THEY NOT HAVE SEEN HIM?

NEELA!

RACING TO HER, HE HAS THE HORRIBLE THOUGHT: THIS WAS HIS FAULT.

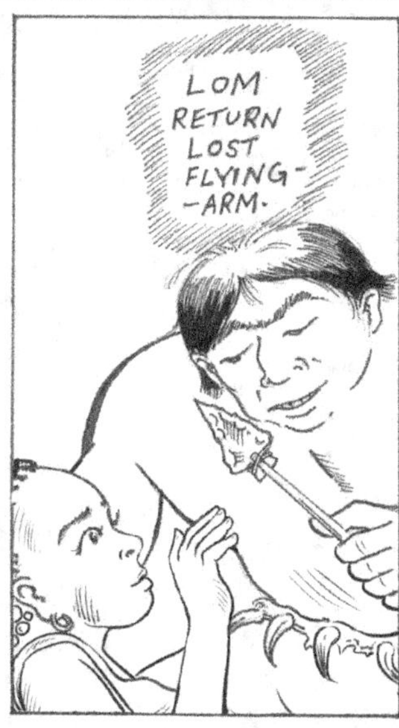

LOM RETURN LOST FLYING-ARM.

NEELA SAFE NOW.
HRONK!
ULP!

NEELA! OH MY GOSH I'M SO SORRY I LEFT YOU! ARE YOU HURT? I SWEAR I'LL...
I'M FINE! LOM AND HIS GIANT PET CAUGHT ME WHEN THE LADDER BROKE!

HIS PET'S NAME IS 'KAJA' -- AND...HERE'S ONE OF YOUR ARROWS! LOM CALLED IT YOUR 'LOST FLYING ARM' (TEE-HEE!)
THAT IS ONE OF MINE -- FROM THE GRYLAR YESTERDAY! BUT WHY WOULD HE...

...HUH?
END OF CHAPTER ONE...

OOUUMPP!
TOLD YOU BEFORE: HANDS OFF THE LADY!
YOU AGAIN? DIDN'T YOU LEARN?
OH, COME ON
COMICS

Brute Issue #2

st notes:

tation: Basically, a ramshackle township on an asteroid circling a sun outside of the milky way.
etically think old westerns or pirate movies except instead of badlands – it's a miniature
scape and some of the architecture is alien-looking. Tars is about 8 blocks squared but more of a
rted double circle filling adjoining craters) with the ship dock on one end (and the medical centre
will eventually end up at the other end).

races: The make-up of species on Tars is very different than Moohoovan Station. The common
s are here – wadrings
                                                        lanterians, McMacs, crystalonians, (no plantis), crabi,
                                                        proon but also mixed with some of the rougher looking
                                                        h, medusas, vuularian.
                                                        rom most of these but medusa's are a corporate-being made
                                                        And as you'd guess, they're snake-like. Tubular with
                                                        lantis vines, they intertwine and arms/legs will be made up
                                                        il) being the 'fingers' or feet. And the 'head' is comprised
                                                        (or even more heads).
t their tails are split into three with each tip further split
hey are more like snails in that their smooth-skinned,
ravel single-file to share the film. The Face isn't at all
scary like for the head. These come in three sizes, very
electric varieties. Each type with their own distinct

BRUTE
TOUGHEST GUY IN THE GALAXY